THE RANGE IS ROUGH, BUT DESK JOBS CAN KILL

Clint was reading yesterday's newspaper and no one had come in looking for a room. Now he knew why so many desk clerks fell asleep on the job.

As Clint turned the pages of the newspaper, the front door opened and a scruffy-looking man entered. He could have just come in from the trail, but somehow Clint doubted it . . .

Without a word the man came to the desk, turned the register around, and began to scan it. Apparently, he found what he wanted because his face lit up like a kid's on Christmas morning.

"Excuse me," Clint said, "Do you want a room?"

"Yeah," the man said. "I want room 212."

Clint turned and looked at the board and saw that room 212 was occupied. When he turned back, the man had produced a shotgun from beneath his long coat. Clint realized then and there that he had made the biggest mistake of his life—and possibly his last.

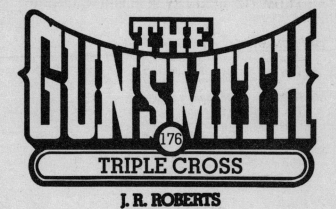

THE GUNSMITH

176

TRIPLE CROSS

J. R. ROBERTS

JOVE BOOKS, NEW YORK

TRIPLE CROSS

A Jove Book / published by arrangement with
the author

PRINTING HISTORY
Jove edition / August 1996

The Putnam Berkley World Wide Web site address is
http://www.berkley.com

ISBN: 0-515-11926-1

A JOVE BOOK®
Jove Books are published by The Berkley Publishing Group,
200 Madison Avenue, New York, New York 10016.
JOVE and the "J" design are trademarks
belonging to Jove Publications, Inc.

PRINTED IN THE UNITED STATES OF AMERICA

10 9 8 7 6 5 4 3 2 1

THE GUNSMITH

176

TRIPLE CROSS

ONE

When Clint Adams spotted the town of Wider's Canyon in the distance it was the first sign of civilization he'd seen in West Texas for days. He'd been riding his big black gelding, Duke, for the better part of a week, enjoying the time of mindless riding he'd been meaning to give himself for a long while.

Clint had lost count of the number of attempts he'd made at rest and relaxation, only to be interrupted by some emergency he couldn't walk away from. So, all he told anyone when he left Labyrinth, Texas, even his good friend Rick Hartman, was that he was going to go wherever Duke took him.

"That's crazy," Hartman said when he first heard of his friend's intention to wander around West Texas for a while.

"I'm telling you, I think I really need to just get away from things," Clint said. "I want to sleep under the stars and not listen to anyone else's problems for a while, that's all."

1

The two were discussing Clint's plans over a cold beer at Rick's saloon, Rick's Place.

"Well, getting away for a while is fine, but at least know where you're going so I can get in touch with you."

Clint just finished his drink, waved good-bye to his friend, and left Labyrinth behind him.

That was days ago.

For now Duke was deciding where and when the two would stop, and he seemed to be headed for Wider's Canyon.

"Getting tired, boy?" Clint asked, patting the gelding's massive neck. "Well, it's too early to call it a day, and I think another night in the fresh air will do us good."

Although he had never been one to turn up his nose at a soft bed and a hot breakfast, Clint was savoring the solitude of the wide open beauty that had brought him to this area.

Looking around and breathing in the warm air, Clint was of a mind to pass up Wider's Canyon altogether. As he approached the outskirts of the small town with the idea of skirting the city limits and moving on, he heard something that attracted his attention.

"Come one, come all and witness the miracle of our century," boomed a deep, rich voice. "Everybody gather round and set your eyes on something that will surely change your lives!"

Clint strained his eyes to see what was going on in what seemed to be the town square. As he inched closer, his curiosity aroused, he could make out the shape of a covered wagon parked in the middle of a growing crowd of excited onlookers.

"That's right, folks," the voice continued, "come and see for yourselves."

His curiosity sufficiently attracted, Clint rode into town just close enough to the action to see what was going on.

Standing on a wooden crate was a man, just under six feet, wearing a black top hat, a dusty gray suit, and a black frock coat.

For a moment, judging by the speaker's wild gestures and dramatic tone, Clint wondered if there was a circus in town. However, written on the side of the man's covered wagon, in large red letters, was: PROFESSOR HENRY WHITEOAK'S AMAZING HEALING ELIXIR. 15¢ TO CURE WHATEVER AILS YOU.

Having seen more than his fair share of snake-oil salesmen in his time, Clint started to turn Duke around to leave town. Before he got started, though, the man standing in front of the wagon began to strut, barking out another line of colorful showmanship that brought another wave of townspeople running.

"Ladies and gentlemen," cried the man in black, "I will cure one of you right before your very eyes. I will do it to prove my all-purpose elixir is genuine . . . and I will do it free of charge, so that everyone can see the astounding powers of my healing tonic!"

Clint couldn't help himself. He had to see this. He brought Duke to a stop at the nearest hitching post, grounded the reins, and joined the crowd.

He peered into the back of the large wagon while continuing to listen to the "professor's" speech. Inside he could see stacks of boxes piled from the floor to the top of the canvas, lining both sides.

"You, sir!"

Clint looked and saw the salesman pointing to an elderly man in the crowd. Gesturing with a silver-tipped cane the speaker urged the old-timer closer to the wagon.

"Yes, you, sir! You look like a man in need of some of the best help modern science has to offer. Come to me and be healed!"

As the scraggly, bearded man made his way forward, Professor Henry Whiteoak did not miss a beat in his presentation.

"All of you good folks will now see the true magic that my miracle tonic can provide. You will all mark this day as the day I, Professor Henry Whiteoak, healed the good town of Wilder Canyon."

Clint looked around to see if anyone had noticed that the good professor had gotten the name of the town wrong, pronouncing it "Wilder" instead of "Wider." What he saw were onlookers who were completely mesmerized by Whiteoak's showy presentation. The man was perhaps the best snake-oil salesman he had ever seen or heard.

The old man picked from the audience was now standing right next to the professor. Clint wondered if the man had deliberately positioned the old-timer beneath the word AMAZING on the side of his wagon.

"Hello there, good sir," Whiteoak said, shaking the man's hand. "And what is your name?"

The man, who looked to be about sixty, with a beat-up face covered with a gnarled, gray beard, gazed nervously at the crowd and then at the tall, black-clad figure next to him.

"My name's Charlie Weathers."

"Well, Charlie, what brings you here today? I know you didn't come just to hear me talk."

Clint shifted his feet and looked at the ground, feeling suddenly foolish. Hearing the salesman's spiel had been all it had taken to pull him away from his trip, which had been going along just fine.

"Speak up, Charlie," Whiteoak said. "We can't hear you."

Apparently the man had mumbled something.

"I said, I got a bad back."

With a flourish and a smile the professor produced a small vial of brown liquid from his coat pocket. Even in the blazing sun of the late afternoon the man managed to look perfectly cool, while the others—Clint included—stewed in the dry, dusty heat.

"My friend," Whiteoak said, "I will present you with this, the answer to your problem, with my compliments, just to show that my intentions are good and true."

Gingerly, Charlie Weathers accepted the small vial, uncorked the top, and raised it to his nose. The man's wrinkled face puckered even more as he sniffed the strange liquid.

The professor laid a hand on Charlie's shoulder.

"It's not going to do you any good just smelling it, my friend. Drink it down." The gawking crowd fell into a hush as he waved his hand theatrically. "Drink it and feel the miracle for yourself."

What happened next was no surprise to Clint. Just as he figured, the old man drank the potion down, shuddered, and began to dance around with the energy of someone half his age. More than likely the old-timer was working with the salesman to make the tonic look good to the crowd.

It worked.

"Whooee!" the old man hooted.

The show and demonstration had served its purpose. As Clint walked back to where Duke was waiting, the townspeople began to flock to Whiteoak's wagon, waving their money. Clint figured the medicine man would make himself a tidy profit this day.

As for himself, what he needed right now was not some miracle tonic to wash his troubles away. Since the better part of the day was behind him and he was already in town, what he needed was a room and a good steak.

He went in search of the livery stable.

TWO

"Can I help you, sir?" asked the scrawny man wearing little round glasses who worked behind the desk of Wider's Room and Board.

"Yes," Clint said. "I'd like a room."

He signed the register as the clerk turned and picked a key from the many hooks on the wall behind him. After handing the key to Clint, the clerk read the name written in the register book.

"Uh . . . Mr. Adams?"

"That's right."

Conversations like this one were why Clint wanted to avoid staying in a town to begin with. At least on the trail nobody recognized him.

"You—you're the Gunsmith, aren't you?"

Clint sighed and glared at the skinny clerk.

"That's not something I'd like to have spread around town," he said. "Do you understand?"

"Uh, yes, sir—"

"What's your name?"

"Alphonse . . . sir."

"Just refer to me as Mr. Adams and we'll get along fine, Alphonse. All right?"

"Uh, yes, sir . . . Mr. Adams."

"Can you tell me where I can get a good steak in this town?"

"We serve dinner in an hour, but Jarvis's place is open. You can eat there . . . Mr. Adams. It's r-right off Main Street."

Without another word Clint went upstairs to his room, put his gear away, and headed back out to search for Jarvis's.

The first thing that caught his eye was the chaos still surrounding Whiteoak's wagon. Men and women were still milling around the colorful wagon, each with a bottle of brown liquid in their hands. Clint shook his head, wondering how so many people could be suckered out of their money so easily. Granted, Whiteoak was good at what he did, but still . . .

With the show over and the crowd breaking up Clint's rumbling stomach took top priority.

"This is just wonderful! My chest has never felt better."

The soft, female voice caught Clint's attention, drawing his focus back to the dispersing crowd.

Clint scanned for the source of the comment and immediately found her. She was tall, almost as tall as Clint himself, with long, straight blonde hair and a face and manner that made it hard for him to tell how old she was. She held herself with the confidence of an older woman, but she had a young girl's enthusiasm. She was dressed in a scoop-necked pink summer dress that showed just a hint of cleavage but still managed to show

off a supple, healthy figure that made Clint give up trying to guess her age.

He also gave up on looking for Jarvis's, for the moment. The lady in pink and her companion, a boy in his
early teens, were headed right for him.

When they got closer Clint could see the blonde taking deep breaths, filling her lungs with air and smiling
as she exhaled. He also noticed how filling her lungs
affected her cleavage, causing it to swell and contract
with every breath.

"I swear my chest pains have been getting worse
every day. Just one sip and I feel fine! I feel like I can
. . . oh, excuse me." She had nearly walked right into
Clint. Of course, he hadn't bothered to move out of her
way.

"That's quite all right, ma'am." He stepped aside and
pointed to the bottle in her hand. "I couldn't help over-
hearing. Is that the miracle tonic I've heard so much
about?"

"Why, yes, it is. Were you here for the demonstration?" she asked.

Before Clint could answer the young boy said, "Professor . . . Professor White-something cured old Mr.
Weathers right in front of the whole town."

Yeah, Clint thought, I'm sure Professor Whiteoak
paid Mr. Weathers well enough to be "cured" in front
of the whole town.

"I just had to buy a bottle for myself," the woman
continued. "I've had chest pains for years and I was just
telling my brother that my chest feels wonderful."

"I'm sure it does," Clint said, trying not to stare at
her chest, which certainly looked wonderful.

"Excuse me?"

"I mean, I'm sure the professor knows what he's doing. Besides, I don't see how there could be anything wrong with you. You seem young and healthy."

The woman had no trouble interpreting the way Clint looked into her eyes with his last comment. She also took a moment to look him over very thoroughly. He was the second stranger to come into town that day, and he was more to her taste than Professor Whiteoak.

"I don't believe I know your name, Mr. . . ." She extended her hand to shake like a man.

"My name is Clint Adams," he said, accepting the hand.

"I'm Marie Groder, and this is my brother, Buck."

The boy looked about fourteen and appeared thin enough to be blown over by a good stiff wind.

"Hello, Buck," Clint said, shaking the boy's hand, as well.

He turned back to Marie and said, "I was just trying to find a place called Jarvis's to get something to eat. Would you like to join me? I mean, both of you?"

"Well . . . I think I . . ." Marie glanced down at her little brother.

"I got things to do," the boy said, clearly getting his sister's message.

"Looks like I'm free for lunch," Marie said to Clint with a smile.

"Good."

Clint smiled and allowed Marie to show him where the restaurant was, two blocks down the street. His bad mood was lifting as he realized his stop in Wider's Canyon might not turn out to be so bad after all.

THREE

Caterville, Texas, was a three-day ride east of Wider's Canyon. The small, dirty town consisted of several run-down structures barely passing for buildings, with too many people trying to live in them. The population was made up of drifters and outlaws, who usually spent no more than a few weeks in the grimy town before they moved on.

Besides being a barren, dangerous place to live, it was a great place to hide out. At least, that was what Frank Morten thought when he first rode into the place two nights ago. After riding hard to get there Morten had been laying low, only venturing out to eat and snatch away one of the whores working Caterville's only saloon.

With his last few nights spent the same way, Morten was itching to leave his cramped hotel room for more than an hour. That itch brought him to the Dead Horse Saloon and kept him there for an all-night poker game. Even though he was about to lose the rest of his pocket money, Morten was feeling better than he had for a long time.

He felt like he could return to normal life. He was beginning to accept the fact that he had actually gotten away with what he'd done.

After throwing down the cards that made up his last losing hand of the night, Morten got up and strutted over to the bar, which was built of five planks set on top of wooden piles. The woman he'd spent every night with since arrival walked over to his side.

"You all through playin', darlin'?" she asked.

"Yeah, I can only lose so much before I need another drink. After that I think we'll be headin' back to my room. Sound good to you, darlin'?"

"Sure," Belle Gristy said. She had attracted his eye because she was the one saloon girl who didn't look totally used up. "You're in a good mood for a man who didn't win a hand all night."

"I'm in a good mood because I think I'll be leavin' this shithole town before too long. As far as money goes, I got enough of that to keep me goin' for a long time."

Morten took a pull from the beer that had been set in front of him by the bartender.

"Yep," he said, half to himself, "for a long time."

After paying for his drink Morten instantly forgot the rusty taste it had left in his mouth. He was too happy to think about things like that. Draping an arm over Belle's shoulder, he leaned over and whispered into her ear.

"How 'bout we celebrate my last night in town?"

With a wink and a smile Belle led the way outside, already planning on how she might be able to relieve Frank Morten of this money she had previously known nothing about.

The couple walked outside onto the rickety board-walk, heading off toward the hotel.

In a dark alley across from the Dead Horse Saloon three men watched as Frank Morten and Belle Gristy came out the door and walked up the street. The men had been waiting there for a few hours longer than they'd expected. After days of watching Morten move about town they'd found his patterns to be etched in stone—until tonight.

Every night he'd venture out of his room, like a rat coming out of its hole, go to the Dead Horse for a meal, and go back with the same ugly whore. Jeremiah Weller was taking his turn watching the saloon when the couple finally made their appearance.

"There they are," he told his partners.

Weller was twenty-five years old, had a body that was as solid as a rock, and was covered with scars that criss-crossed his face and torso. Wearing a bowie knife and a .45 strapped to his hip, he always looked ready for a fight.

The man who came to his side at the sound of his voice looked like he could have been Weller's brother. A few years older, and every bit as intimidating as the other man, Luke Kylie had the rugged look of experience burning behind his dark eyes. Standing an inch shorter than Weller, Kylie was a bit lankier than Weller, but made up for his lesser strength by carrying a shotgun as well as a Colt Peacemaker beneath his battered duster.

The larger man had a reputation for taking men apart with his bare hands, while Kylie did the same using the shotgun. Peering into the night Luke spotted the pair making their way back to the hotel.

"He's still got that same old whore with him," he

complained. "Should we take him anyway?"

The team had observed Morten for the past few days, allowing the man to think he was safe, thereby lowering his guard. The third man thought that Morten would be even more vulnerable with the woman. They'd literally catch him with his pants down.

"Yeah," he said to the other two, "let's take 'im."

FOUR

Frank Morten pulled Belle into his room, closing the door behind them. The woman's experienced hands felt their way down his body, over his stomach, down to his crotch, groping his already-hard cock. Her tongue probed into his mouth as she stroked him through his pants.

Pushing her away from him, Morten pulled the dress from her body, exposing her large, sweaty breasts. They were full and round with large brown nipples hardening as the air hit them. As usual, Belle wasn't wearing any underwear. Scanning every inch of her plump yet solid body, Morten's eyes fell to the soft patch between her legs.

Belle knelt down in front of him, pulled his pants to the floor, and held him in her hand. As though she were enjoying a stick of candy, she ran her tongue over him, from the base to the tip, while cupping his balls in her hand. She repeated the motion again before taking him fully into her mouth. Still using her tongue while she sucked him, Belle's head rocked back and forth, pushing

15

Morten to the point where he could wait no longer.

She recognized this and slowly backed away from him, moving toward the bed. Sitting on the edge of the bed, facing him, the woman spread her legs open just the way she knew he liked it. Putting her hand to her mouth, she licked one of her fingers and added that moisture to her own by rubbing her clit slowly . . . hungrily. As she stroked herself she could feel her own desires rising to a boil. The hot wetness between her legs was increasing, and she wanted to feel the man inside of her.

"Come on, Frank," she moaned. "Come and get it."

Morten didn't miss a beat. In one motion he all but jumped on top of the prostitute, his rigid cock still glistening with her saliva. He reached down and guided his shaft into her, plunging hard and fast. She moaned as he entered her and wrapped her arms around his back, digging into his skin with her fingernails.

"That's it," she growled into his ear, "fuck me . . . fuck me hard!"

His pace quickened as she spoke to him. He reached beneath her and grabbed her buttocks, using his grip to pull her to him. Belle's legs came up around him now and held him close while he pounded himself into her steamy depths.

Before too long Morten could feel his passion building to its climax. He felt the tidal wave rising up inside, getting ready to explode out and into the woman he was riding like a bucking bronco.

Before he could build to his shattering climax, though, Morten's door was suddenly kicked in, and three men entered.

"What the hell—" Morten yelled, rolling off of Belle and onto the floor.

Luke Kylie swung an arm up from beneath his duster, leveling the shotgun at the bed. Before Morten could say another word the weapon's roar filled the room and fire seem to leap from the barrel. The blast took a large chunk out of the bed's flimsy headboard and an even larger chunk out of Belle Gristy's body.

"Hello, Frank," said the leader of the trio while the smoke still curled from Luke's shotgun. "Now that I have your undivided attention, we have a little business to discuss with you."

FIVE

Frank Morten stared at the bed, shaking like a leaf from the blast that had torn apart the woman he'd been having sex with just seconds before. The smell of her scorched skin was still fresh in his nose as he looked at her dead body. Slowly, his eyes turned to the men who stood just inside the door.

Luke Kylie leveled his shotgun at Morten while the trio's leader strutted further into the room, followed by Jeremiah Weller. The leader of the men was six foot one, with smooth, pale skin and a black, bushy mustache covering the better part of his mouth. He wore a gray suit, silver-tipped boots, and a black dress coat that concealed a double-rig shoulder holster.

"Who—who're you?" Morten stammered.

"My name," he said, "is John Duggin."

Morten's eyes widened.

"You're John Duggin . . . John 'The Killer' Duggin?" Morten made no effort to hide his fear of the man standing in front of him.

18

Weller unsheathed his bowie knife and pressed the tip to Morten's throat.

"Did you really think you could run and hide from us after what you pulled on Mr. Halsey?" he demanded.

"It w-was all a b-big mistake," Morten stammered. "I s-swear I never m-meant to—"

Duggin waved away Morten's words with an impatient flick of his hand.

"Save the pleading and shut the hell up, you pathetic little bastard. You try to swindle Mr. Halsey out of his land interests in half the ranches he owns in New Mexico, run off and hide here losing his money in poker and spending it on ugly whores, and then expect us to believe it was an accident?"

Morten surprised himself by thinking that Belle hadn't been all that ugly. He must have been so scared he wasn't even thinking rationally.

"I'll tell you where you made your mistake," Duggin went on. "Your big mistake was in picking such a piss-poor place to hide out."

Weller removed the knife blade from under Morten's chin, allowing him to scramble to his feet to face the men, so frightened that he literally forgot that he was naked.

"Please, Mr. Duggin. Just let me go, and I'll give you everything I got and disappear. Nobody'll know. You can say you lost me."

Duggin's eyes seemed to stare right through the pleading man's head. Turning to his partners he motioned to them to put their weapons away and leave him alone with Morten. The two killers placed their weapons back in hiding and left the hotel room, closing the door behind them. If anyone responded to the sound of the shotgun blast, they'd take care of them, no matter who it was.

Luckily, Caterville had little in the way of law.

"I'll tell you what," Duggin said, when they were alone. "Show me what you got to offer and we'll see what kind of a deal we can come up with."

Morten's eyes brightened with hope as he started toward his saddlebags, which contained all of his possessions and money. When he turned around with his offering in his hands, he found Duggin facing him with his long black coat open, revealing the twin .45's. One was still in its holster, while the other was in Duggin's right hand.

The naked man didn't even get to say a word before the first shot erupted from Duggin's pistol. The slug tore through Morten's left hip, spinning his body around and sending him crashing to the floor.

A little smile crept onto Duggin's face at the sight of the naked man's face as the bullet struck him just when his hopes for escape were at their peak. Enthralled in a passion caused by the sight of the man's blood, Duggin quickly blew two more holes into Frank Morten . . . one in the leg, the other in his belly.

When Morten's eyes looked helplessly into those of "Killer" Duggin, pleading for mercy, the little smile on Duggin's face turned into a smirk, and then a wide grin at the sight of the other man flopping around on the floor in a pool of his own blood.

Duggin waited for the look of pain to fully register on Morten's face before he knelt down at the man's side. He wanted to hear anything that Morten had to say, any sound that he might make as death crept up to him. That was part of the pleasure for him.

"Tell Mr. Halsey . . ." Morten croaked, "tell him . . . to kiss my . . . ass."

"I will, Frank."

Duggin pulled the trigger one more time, sending a single bullet through Morten's left eye and out the back of his head.

"Good-bye, Frank."

Standing, John Duggin couldn't help but allow his grin to take over his entire face. While the sheer joy of taking another man's life washed over him, he looked like a kid who had just awakened on Christmas morning.

Just for the hell of it he blew one more hole into Morten's head, reaching for one more second of pleasure, but it just wasn't the same.

He opened the door and strolled out into the hallway, carrying Morten's saddlebags. He'd dumped the man's belongings on the floor and put the papers back in.

"Come on, boys," he said. "Let's get out of this shithole town."

The three men made their way to their horses, which were saddled and ready, and started back toward Joe Halsey's place, which was four days' ride north of Caterville. They encountered no law, or anyone for that matter, to question them about the shooting.

To the citizens of Caterville, Frank Morten was just another poor, dead bastard who probably got what was coming to him.

SIX

Like the rest of Wider's Canyon, Jarvis's was nothing that Clint hadn't seen in plenty of other towns. When he and Marie Groder walked through the doors, the place was about half full. There were a dozen tables with mainly families or couples occupying them.

A few minutes after they sat down, a hefty man in his thirties took their order. Clint asked for a steak and Marie had the same.

Looking across at the attractive blonde, Clint couldn't help but notice how well she filled out her low-cut dress.

"So, have you lived in Wider's Canyon your whole life?" he asked her.

"Yes. I've never been farther than Coogan's Bluff. That's just a day's ride north. My uncle Ben lives there."

"I probably would have wound up there if I hadn't stopped here," Clint said. "I really wasn't planning on coming through town."

"What changed your mind?"

"I heard the professor and got curious," Clint said, and then explained what his intentions had been with his traveling.

"That sounds exciting," she said, leaning forward and revealing more cleavage. "I've always wanted to travel." She folded her hands on the table and looked down at them. "We hardly ever see any strangers come through this place. Then today, all of a sudden, we get two, you and Professor Whiteoak."

Looking into the small-town girl's sparkling blue eyes Clint had just about forgotten the flamboyant "medicine man" whose spiel had drawn him into town. Maybe he'd have occasion to thank the man.

Their steaks arrived, and after setting them down their server produced his bottle of the miracle tonic. Marie's bottle was on the table.

"Guess you two saw that Whiteoak fella, huh?" he said, not waiting for them to respond. "I got me some of this here elixir, too, and my back pains have just about disappeared."

Marie nodded enthusiastically.

"I got some, too, and it did wonders for my chest," she said.

Clint wondered how much of this was mind over matter, and how much of it was the alcohol that was undoubtedly one of the ingredients.

"How about you?" the server asked him.

"No. I saw the show but I don't, uh, have any ailments that need curing." He knew that a salesman was a salesman, but he didn't want to burst these people's bubble, not if they actually were feeling better. Maybe Whiteoak was doing them a service after all.

"Well, Clint, you can try some of mine, if you like,"

Marie offered. "The professor said it even helps your food digest."

He smiled at her and said, "My food digests just fine, Marie, but thanks for the offer. I might need it later from the looks of this steak, though."

With that remark the waiter left in a huff. Apparently he was also the cook.

Marie laughed before picking up her silverware and starting on the meal.

"If you want," she said, "I could check in on you later. I mean—you know, to see if you changed your mind . . . about the tonic, I mean." She looked up at Clint, somewhat embarrassed but not ashamed.

Clint took a bite of the steak, gnawed on the gristly beef, and made a face.

"That's probably a good idea."

Again Marie laughed. The action made her face look as though it had been lit up by a ray of sunshine. When Clint told her where he could be found later in the evening, her smile subsided into a guilty little smirk. Clint could tell that she didn't make a habit of meeting with strange men.

The two finished their meal with more small talk. When they walked back outside, into the night air, Marie rested her hands on Clint's shoulders and looked right into his eyes. When she spoke it was in a rich, sultry voice she hadn't used all evening.

"I've got some errands to run, but I'll see you later. And . . ." she said, kissing him gently on the lips, "thanks for dinner."

"You're very welcome."

As Clint watched her walk down the street he saw her in a new light. He saw a woman walking away like she knew a man was watching her. Maybe she wasn't the small-town little innocent that he thought she was.

Oh, well, he thought as he headed toward the saloon, all the better.

SEVEN

The sprawling ranch on the eastern boundary of Fort Tesson, Texas, was the source of many deals. The most recent business transaction had just been completed by the three men who rode up to the ranch's main house and dismounted their horses.

Fresh from the trail, John Duggin, Jeremiah Weller, and Luke Kylie brushed the grit from their clothes and strode up to the house's front porch. They were greeted by one of the many ranch hands, who took charge of their horses. They knocked on the front door and were greeted there by a black houseman, who took their coats and showed them into a comfortable study. He even brought them some water to clear the dust from the back of their throats. Drinks would probably be offered by the master of the house.

The walls of the study were lined with photographs of various other properties. Weller and Kylie found them fascinating, as neither had seen many photos before. There were cattle ranches, horse ranches, and even small towns pictured there. The man who would soon occupy the chair behind the enormous oak desk owned everything in the grainy photographs. He was a man who wanted nothing more than to acquire all that he could. He wanted to control anyone and anything that he could. That meant owning land.

Joseph Halsey was one of the biggest landowners in this part of the country—possibly in all of Texas and New Mexico. Besides owning the places in the photographs on his wall, he also controlled the lives of those who lived there. One thing he did not abide was being crossed by one of those people . . . or anyone else.

That was where the three men sitting in the study came in handy. They were his personal troubleshooters. For Halsey, Frank Morten had been trouble. The rest was up to Duggin and his men.

The assassins had been waiting for about ten minutes when Halsey finally entered the room. Standing six feet three inches, he looked down at the killers with cold, scheming eyes. His body betrayed his soft life-style, as others did most of the manual labor for him, but his face showed no sign of weakness.

"So, tell me that Morten has been taken care of," he said to John Duggin. He ignored the other two men. They were ignorant and simply did as they were told by Duggin, who was the one with the brains.

The leader of the killers said, "Offer us a drink."

Weller and Kylie never understood what went on between Duggin and Halsey. The men were forever fencing with each other, pushing to see how far they could push.

Halsey went to a small sideboard and poured three glasses of brandy without asking who wanted one. He handed a glass to each of the three men, who accepted happily.

While Weller and Kylie drank deeply, Duggin considered the man he worked for over the rim of his glass.

"Yeah," he said finally, "Morten's dead. He tried hiding out for a while, but we found him. We kept an eye on him for a few days before we made our move."

"Why'd you wait so long?" Halsey asked, seating himself behind the luxurious desk. The sturdy wood of his chair creaked under his bulk as he leaned forward to stare at Duggin. "I told you to kill him quick, so he wouldn't get a chance to hide my property. Did you at least find what I told you to find?"

Duggin's eyes narrowed to fiery slits when the big Texan raised his voice. Shifting in their seats, Weller and Kylie were ready to back whatever play their leader's temper might lead to. Without question, their loyalties were to John Duggin and no one else.

"Look, Halsey, I'm not one of your ranch hands, so you'd better watch how you talk to me. As far as I'm concerned, you're just another paycheck. You're a big paycheck, but you'll be an even bigger corpse if you don't watch yourself."

Leaning back in his chair, Halsey smiled at the three men. It was precisely because he *was* a big paycheck that he didn't quite take Duggin's threats seriously. It was more than likely that the man was simply posturing for the benefit of his men.

"You know, Duggin, that's why I hired you. You've got the guts to stand up to me like that. Now, did you get them or not?"

Duggin motioned to the man sitting to his right, which

was Luke Kylie. At the signal Kylie reached into his duster and pulled out a stack of papers, tied together with a piece of twine. With the tension between the two bosses still crackling in the air, Kylie left his coat open, leaving his shotgun free, when he put the papers into Duggin's waiting hand.

"Here you go, fat man," Duggin said, tossing the papers onto Halsey's desk where they landed with an audible thud. "Don't choke on 'em."

Halsey snatched up the bundle and quickly snapped the twine, keeping the papers together. As he flipped through the documents he nodded his approval. Each sheet was a deed to a spread of property that Frank Morten had stolen and made off with a week ago. The deeds, a few of Halsey's hundreds, were missed in two days' time. Soon after Duggin was called in, Morten was found and the assassins were back . . . mission accomplished.

The Texan behind the desk opened a drawer and filed away the recovered papers.

"Morten said this land belonged to his family at one time," he said.

"Did it?" Duggin asked.

"I don't give a shit," Halsey said. "It's mine now, and he stole it."

"Speaking of what's yours," Duggin said, "I believe we're here to collect some of your money that's now rightfully ours."

The land baron reached into a different drawer and produced a small, leather pouch. After feeling its weight in his hand one final time he tossed it over to Duggin.

"It's all there, John, in gold, just the way you like it."

The killer opened the bag to inspect the contents. Satisfied, he stuck it into an inside pocket of his coat, snug against the shoulder rig. With another motion to his men the assassins were on their feet and headed for the door. Weller and Kylie left their empty glasses on the desk, while Duggin's glass was still full. He hated Halsey's expensive brandy.

"Hold up there, boy," Halsey said as they started to leave.

The words stopped Duggin dead in his tracks. Slowly he turned to face the big Texan.

"I . . . ain't . . . your . . . boy," he said slowly. Kylie and Weller stood aside, waiting to see if lead would fly.

Without flinching Halsey struck a match and lit the cigar he produced from his shirt pocket.

"How'd you like to earn triple that amount for another job? Maybe more?"

With those words some of the fire went out of Duggin's eyes.

"What?"

Halsey took a moment to light the cigar before continuing.

"I said I got another job for you boys that pays triple what you got for killing Morten. If you do a good enough job, there might even be more in it for you."

Glancing over at both of his partners, Duggin checked for their approval, not that he really needed it. He made all of the decisions for the three of them, but he always checked with them, anyway, to see what they thought. In their line of work their lives were at risk with every job they took.

"Want to sit back down?" Halsey asked.

"Just talk," Duggin said.

"I've been hearing about an old acquaintance of mine

showing his face not too far from here. Remember those ranches I bought last year that wound up being a bunch of rocky fields next to a dried-up river?''

Duggin smiled. ''Yeah.'' He had enjoyed the idea of Halsey, the big land baron, being taken.

''Well, the guy who sold 'em to me was a prime con man who disappeared after swindling me out of a whole lot of money. He was better at runnin' and hidin' than ol' Frank Morten, but I hear he's up to his old tricks again, in the western part of the state.''

Halsey took a few puffs from his cigar, rolling the smoke around in his mouth before going on.

''His name's Henry Whiteoak. Him and the men who helped him pull the wool over my eyes are all starting to appear again, thinkin' they're safe. I want you to find them and show them that they aren't.''

''How many of them are there?'' Duggin asked.

''Five and Whiteoak, himself.'' Halsey tossed a piece of paper on the desk. ''Their names are written down there, along with the last place they were seen. You kill the five and bring me Whiteoak, alive. I want to look into his lyin' eyes one more time before he dies. You do that and I'll make the three of you rich.''

Duggin leaned forward, stroking his mustache.

''There's six of them and you only want to pay us triple?'' he asked.

''None of them are gunmen,'' Halsey said, ''but don't worry, I'll make it worth your while.'' He stuck the cigar in his mouth and spoke around it. ''What do you say?''

''We'll let you know,'' Duggin said, standing up. ''We'll let you know by tomorrow if we refuse. If you

don't hear from us . . .'' the killer said, with a smirk as
he thought of how he'd kill the five men, ''then you can
wait for us to arrive with that Whiteoak fella. The others
you'll have to read about in the obituaries.''

EIGHT

The Diamondback Saloon wasn't Wider's Canyon's only saloon, but it was the only one Clint Adams had spotted since his arrival in town. The place resembled every other rickety building he'd seen that day, looking like it had been built in one day with reused wood that was never that good to begin with. As he opened the front door, the large wooden plank seemed ready to fall off its hinges.

Inside there were no surprises either. To his left was a long wooden bar which he was sure had seen its fair share of bumps, crashes, and gunshot wounds. To his right he saw four gaming tables, only two of which had house dealers. The house-run games were poker and blackjack. The other two tables were poker games being played and run privately.

Amid all the loud talking and the sound of a lone piano player in the back of the place, Clint heard one familiar voice booming over all the others. Looking around for the source, his eyes finally came to rest on one of the private poker games. Sure enough, the current dealer of that game was Henry Whiteoak.

Clint walked over to the bar. The burly barkeep walked over to him and stared at his face for a few seconds before saying a word.

"Another stranger, huh?"

Clint stared straight back at the man's leathery face. The bartender was in his fifties but was built like the kind of guy that could take a man's best punch without even flinching. In the back of his mind Clint hoped he'd hold up as well when he was older.

"Yeah," Clint said, "I just got here today. Nice little town you've got here."

"You're kiddin', right?"

Clint didn't answer.

"What'll ya have?"

"Beer."

When the barman returned with a cold mug Clint sipped at it, wondering why he didn't just up and leave Wider's Canyon and spend the night under the stars again. Then the sweet face of Marie Groder filled his thoughts. With that, the situation didn't seem so bad. He knew she'd be calling on him later on, and he hoped she had the same thing in mind that he did. He decided to kill some time over a nice simple game of poker before heading back to his hotel.

"The name's Jack Carson," the bartender said, surprising Clint by extending his hand. The man also allowed a smile to crack his stony face.

"Clint Adams."

"Adams . . . heard of ya. Welcome to Wider's Canyon, Mr. Adams. Sorry if I was . . . gruff. I ain't had such a great day."

"It's tough running a business like this."

"You said it. Passin' through?"

"I was passing by when I heard what was going on in the street."

The bartender frowned a moment, then said, "Oh, you mean that Whiteoak fella."

"That's right."

Carson shook his head.

"Fella strikes me as the type trouble follows," he said. "Look at him now. Not only did he take money off of everybody for his tonic, but he's been beating them at poker. Sooner or later somebody's gonna get mad."

"Did you try any of his tonic?"

"You know, I did, just to see what it was like, and you know what?"

"What?"

Carson pulled a bottle of whiskey from behind the bar.

"I think people would feel just as good if they drank some of this with a little laudanum."

"That's all that stuff is?"

"That's all I taste," Carson said. "Hell, all my troubles used to go away when I drank this stuff, too, that's why I stopped." Carson jerked his head toward the poker game. "He may put on a better show, but we're peddlin' the same stuff."

"And you don't mind?"

"Hell, he'll be gone in a day or two, and when people run out of his stuff, they'll come runnin' right back here."

"Well," Clint said, "he does put on a good show, I'll give him that. I think I'll go over and see what kind of poker player he is."

Carson, fully aware of who Clint was and of his rep-

utation, smiled knowingly as he watched Clint head over
to Whiteoak's poker game. He wished he had the time
to just stand and watch the Gunsmith take on the con
man . . . even if it was just in a game of poker.

NINE

As Clint approached the poker game, one of the players pushed his chair away from the table and went walking off, not looking very happy. That left a vacant seat.

"Mind if I sit in?" he asked.

No one objected, and Whiteoak smiled broadly and said, "Not at all, sir. Happy to have some fresh blood in the game, eh, gents?"

"He's been takin' money from all of us, mister," one of the other players said. "Just so ya know."

"I'll take my chances," Clint said, taking the vacated seat and setting some bills on the table.

As Whiteoak collected his winnings and the next man shuffled the cards, Clint got his first good look at the medicine man. He appeared to be in his mid-to late thirties, with a slender body and face, distinguished by a sharp, prominent chin. His skin was pale and seemed even more so in contrast to the black outfits he always wore.

Dressed in the traditional gambler's black suit and

string tie, he had the look of a proper gentleman. Besides Clint he was the only man who looked as if he'd had a bath and shave in the past week. Clint had had one in a stream just two days earlier.

Clint guessed that his whisker-free face made him look a bit younger than he really was.

Clint noticed one other thing about the so-called professor. He had a confident air about him, probably reflecting a belief that he could handle anything that came along. If he was the kind of man Clint thought he was, he'd need that kind of self-confidence to survive.

When Whiteoak had sorted his paper and coins, the dealer began the next hand.

"This is a friendly draw poker game," Whiteoak said, "so we should all be acquainted. I am Professor Henry Whiteoak and this gentleman dealing the cards is Tom Middles."

Middles looked over and nodded his head, acknowledging Clint's presence while showing no feelings about it one way or another. He was a young man in his early twenties. Clint guessed that the man's scraggly mustache was an attempt to add some years to his appearance. With his simple clothes and blank stare Clint figured him for a ranch hand. He didn't figure a man that young would have his own spread.

"And this other fellow on your right is George Golder."

Golder gave a short wave to Clint. A large man in his fifties, Golder had the look of a local businessman or merchant. His brown suit, worn and sweated through from his day's work, didn't do a good job of hiding the fat body underneath. The older man's face was covered with a thick, well-trimmed beard, and rather than having a blank look his face seemed friendly . . . or perhaps bemused. It had been he who warned Clint that Whiteoak was winning.

"And that gent to your left," Whiteoak finished, "is Dan Hefner."

Hefner was in his thirties, clean shaven and tired-looking. Like Middles he had the look of a ranch hand, and as he picked up his cards Clint saw that his hands and fingers were scarred. More than likely he worked with horses and had been bitten his fair share of times. In fact, he had a scar on his left cheek that resembled a bite mark.

"And you are?" Whiteoak asked.

"My name's Clint," he said. "I just got here today."

"As did I, sir, and a fine little town it is, too," Whiteoak announced. "Passing through?"

"I am, and I thought this game might help me pass some time."

"Ah, time is not something that should be passed, sir," Whiteoak said. "It is something that should be savored and squeezed for everything you can get from it."

Clint looked at the other men, who rolled their eyes and wore the expressions of people who'd been listening to that kind of talk long before he joined the game.

"Yes, well," Clint said, "I guess you're right."

"Can we play cards?" Hefner asked, annoyed. Apparently he was not taking the constant losing very well.

Clint picked up his five cards and spread them in his hands. He had an ace, three, and jack of hearts, along with the two of clubs and the king of spades.

Middles started the betting by throwing two dollars into the middle of the table. With these stakes, Clint thought, he was glad that he was just playing to play and not to win serious money.

Clint tossed in his money and Hefner and Golder did

the same. Whiteoak raised a dollar before the players'
cards were discarded and the replacements were dealt
out. Clint threw away his two cards, the two and the
king, going for the flush. In a higher stakes game he
might have just folded, but he was here to play. He got
one more heart, the six, and the ace of diamonds.

Close, but no good.

The betting went on until there was a fairly decent
pot in the middle of the table. When the hands were laid
down and shown, Middles wound up with two pairs,
eights and threes; Golder had a straight; Clint had aces;
Hefner three fives; and Whiteoak a flush to win the hand.

"Looks like the spades get it," Whiteoak said. "Well
played, gentlemen, well played."

There wasn't much in the way of agreement from the
others at the table.

The deal passed to Golder, and as he shuffled, Whiteoak looked across the table at Clint and fiddled with his
string tie.

"You didn't tell us your last name, Clint."

Clint hesitated, then said, "Adams."

"Clint Adams," Whiteoak repeated. "I believe I've
heard of you."

Clint, who had been feeling good about being able to
sit in on a poker game without anyone knowing who he
was, looked up from his folded hands and waited for the
professor to continue. None of the other men said anything, whether they recognized his name or not.

Whiteoak raised a hand to his chin, rubbing his
smooth skin as he thought. Clint felt it was an act. The
man knew perfectly well who he was.

"I know," he said finally, "you were a lawman once,
weren't you?"

"That was a long time ago," Clint said. Whiteoak

was younger than he was. He was sure *that* wasn't what the man remembered, but for some reason he wanted to play it that way.

"Well," Whiteoak said, "I knew I knew you from someplace."

As Golder dealt the next hand, Whiteoak stared for a few seconds at Clint before speaking again.

"Actually, I knew a man named Adams once," he said. "I met him when I was up in the Oklahoma Territory. I was there to help the poor people there during a terrible drought. But that was a long time ago, when I was still adept at the ancient Indian art of rainmaking. I have a good story to go along with that. This man and I were working on the clouds, and he had a daughter . . ."

TEN

Later, Clint managed to pull three jacks only to be beaten by Whiteoak's three kings. Golder and Hefner had dropped out, but Middles had stayed with a pair of aces. Apparently, the boy didn't realize he was in over his head. Clint didn't know if anyone else even noticed, but he recognized Whiteoak for the professional gambler that he was.

The professor, every time he received his turn to deal, never failed to shuffle and do so with a flourish. Every motion the man made was a show in itself. As much as he hated to admit it, Clint couldn't help but be amused and entertained by the man. He rarely shut up, but his countless stories and anecdotes suited Clint just fine, as they helped pass the time.

An hour after Clint had arrived, Golder stood up from the table.

"I'll be back, fellas," he said. "Call of nature."

Whiteoak turned his attention to the young man on his left.

"So tell me, Tom," he said, fanning the cards out on the table with one sweeping motion, "do you gamble much?"

Clint had begun to enjoy the spectacle that Whiteoak had turned the game into. Normally, Clint took his poker very seriously, but he was coming out even, so he thought he'd sit back and watch Whiteoak's displays and listen to his stories until he started to lose, or until he was in danger of missing his meeting with Marie.

The young man shifted in his seat as he thought about how to respond to Whiteoak's question. Putting on a tough look, Middles puffed out his chest and said, "Yeah, I gamble. Why? You got somethin' to say about the way I play?"

"Just make sure you don't gamble with your food money, that's all," Whiteoak said.

"Whataya, worried I'll take your money?"

Whiteoak simply shook his head and continued flipping the cards around in his hands. Clint noticed that in the one-handed shuffle the top card never changed.

Clint knew what the question was meant to be, and was surprised to hear Whiteoak asking it. It was a professional gambler giving an amateur a warning. He was telling the boy that he knew Middles didn't gamble well and to think about what he was doing with his money. On the other hand the amateur had no way of seeing the statement as anything other than a taunt.

Clint had to admire Whiteoak for giving the boy the warning. For all of the stories and bluster the medicine man was full of, Clint had come to the conclusion that he was, indeed, a character, and a likeable one at that.

But he also had the feeling that Whiteoak was something else, though he wasn't fully ready to believe it, yet.

George Golder returned and said, "Okay, boys, let's play poker."

They played for another hour before Clint finally had to admit that he saw the pattern. After he noticed that Whiteoak's luck seemed to go beyond what fate would allow, he started to watch the man carefully. While the man won his fair share of hands dealt by other players, he always managed to win the hands he dealt, himself.

Four hands later Clint was able to see that he was, indeed, right. Whiteoak was dealing the hand, and while he dealt the first four cards the top card in the deck never changed. In fact, it was highly possible that Whiteoak was also palming cards to be used later in the game. If he was, he was so good that Clint couldn't spot him. He did, however, spot the man cheating while he was dealing.

At this point Clint had three choices. He could stay and lose the rest of his money, bit by bit. He could call Whiteoak the cheater that he was, which would probably get the man killed.

His third choice was to simply walk away, and this was the one he decided on.

Although Whiteoak was apparently a cheater *and* a con man, Clint didn't want to see the man killed for it. Hell, he thought, a lot of people cheated at cards. Whiteoak just happened to get caught at it.

At the end of the hand, while the professor was raking in his winnings, Clint pushed away from the table. Amazingly, he was still even.

"That's it for me."

"Oh, but the night is young, Clint," Whiteoak said. "Don't you want a chance to win your money back?"

Clint stared straight ahead into the other man's eyes.

"Something tells me that's not going to happen, Professor."

Without another word Clint stood up and left the table and went over to the bar. He could not tell from the look in Whiteoak's eyes whether the man knew he had been caught or not.

All in all he felt that he had accomplished what he'd set out to do. He'd killed a couple of hours playing cards, listened to a lot of tall tales and dirty jokes, and had not lost any money. In fact, after he counted he discovered that he had actually won a few dollars.

At the bar he ordered his second beer of the night and decided to leave the saloon after he finished it. Just as he was preparing to leave the saloon, though, Clint heard a commotion coming from the poker table. He stopped in his tracks to listen to the ruckus.

"You're a lyin' cheat!" a man's voice said.

"Yeah! You was cheatin' us the whole time, you bastard!" another voice said.

Clint identified the first voice as that of Dan Hefner and the second as Tom Middles. Obviously, they had somehow stumbled on to the fact that Henry Whiteoak had been cheating. He was tempted to keep going as someone overturned the poker table, to mind his own business, but if he did that Henry Whiteoak might end up getting killed.

"Aw, hell," he said, and turned toward the commotion. First Whiteoak's flamboyance had drawn him into town, and now it was getting him into a fight.

ELEVEN

Joe Halsey stared out of the massive window of his study to survey his domain. In the back of his mind he knew there was a lot more of his land out there that he couldn't see. Thinking about all of the countless ranches, farms, towns, and undeveloped acres still waiting to be used, Halsey began to feel all warm inside. It was one of the few things that gave him any joy.

Then his thoughts drifted to a little place called Callerwood, Oklahoma. When he'd first heard the name he was assured the land was rich, the people were hard workers, and the cattle were plentiful, like water in the river.

He had been skeptical, at first, but the man who told him the stories produced witnesses ranging from the town's mayor to one of Halsey's own land scouts, who all backed up the testimony a hundred percent.

After Halsey bought the ranches surrounding the town for a large sum of money, all of the men vanished . . . including his own scout. The ranches turned out to be deserted and used up, the river was dry, and the town consisted of six rat-infested buildings that were ready to fall down at any time.

He'd been taken in by a clever con man.

Worse than that, everybody knew about it. The news spread like wildfire, and Halsey was certain people were laughing at him behind his back. That was something he could not tolerate.

Now, while he looked out his window, he knew that Duggin and his men were out there. They were hunting down those men who had made a fool of him. When they brought back the stinking bastard who planned the whole thing, Halsey would kill him personally.

"You can run, Henry Whiteoak," Halsey said in a low rumble, "but you aren't going to get away from me."

John Duggin, feeling the rush of the wind over his body and the vibrations of the horse beneath him, thought about how he would kill the first man they were going after once they found him. Whiteoak and his partners would not be difficult to locate. All of the men were gamblers and swindlers, neither of which would or could go unnoticed for very long. Those kinds of men had to get back on the con as soon as possible. They had no choice.

The assassins only had to hunt for one day before they found someone who recognized one of the pictures drawn by one of Joe Halsey's ranch hands, who had seen all of the con men. Duggin knew there would be no shortage of men wanting the swindlers to be caught. All he had to do was let it be known he was looking and someone would speak up.

That was all it took to find Sage Johnson.

Sage was a run-of-the-mill card hustler who hooked up with Whiteoak for an occasional job. Now, according to the man Duggin had talked to yesterday, Sage was in a town two days' ride away. Apparently, Sage had barely escaped death at the hands of the very man who pointed Duggin in the right direction. That man had no reservations about sending a professional killer after the target he himself had missed.

Duggin and his men had been riding all day long. He figured they'd get to Running Water, Oklahoma, early the next morning. Not wanting to waste any time Duggin planned on leaving that same night, before anyone even had a chance to find Sage's body.

With a renewed feeling of urgency, Duggin drove his horse on. John "The Killer" Duggin loved his work and wanted to get on with it.

Although Running Water, Oklahoma, was not Sage Johnson's idea of a lively town, it did have its fair share of saloons—there were three of them—and the swindler had no problem plying his crooked trade. He'd been fleecing patrons of the Royal Lady Gaming Hall for some time at a crooked faro table. The players, he suspected, were beginning to catch on to him, so his operations would soon be moving down the street to the Broken Back Saloon.

That, however, would not be until next week. Until then Johnson planned on milking his little scam for all he could. Thoughts of his next business venture were swarming through Johnson's mind as he prepared himself for his day at work.

He dressed in a black suit with a white shirt. Although it was almost unbearably hot this afternoon, he still wore the suit jacket to provide the pockets he needed to store his Colt revolver and throwing knife.

With a cocky pride in his step, Johnson made his way down to the lobby and out of his hotel. In a few minutes he was in his familiar place behind the back table of the Royal Lady, dealing faro.

''All right,'' he said to the men milling around the gaming table, waiting for the dealer to arrive, ''let's get down to business.''

As he dealt the first hand of the night Johnson felt good. He had that warm feeling he got in his gut when he knew he was onto something sweet. Johnson knew he was playing his cards right in Running Water. He was laying relatively low and staying smart.

At this pace he'd have another month or two in this town before he had to leave . . . voluntarily, or otherwise. In the back of his mind he knew he still had to watch his back. His last job gave him a powerful enemy, besides a sackful of money.

All in all, everything was going according to plan. Johnson started his night's work with his spirits ignorantly high and a smile on his face.

TWELVE

Henry Whiteoak stared straight down the barrel of Dan Hefner's six-shooter as he lay on the floor, next to the overturned poker table. After Clint Adams had left the game, the three other poker players began to wonder why Whiteoak's winning streak had become so strong. Like Clint, they found out why. Unlike Clint, they weren't going to let him get away with it.

"Come now, Dan," Whiteoak said. "Let's settle this like responsible adults."

"Shoot 'im!" Tom Middles shouted.

"That's what I'm plannin' to do," Hefner said. Clint didn't know if Hefner was responding to what Whiteoak said, or what Middles said. The man stepped forward and pressed the barrel of his gun to Whiteoak's sweaty brow.

From his position next to Hefner, Tom Middles watched the scene with a nervous smile. The young man hadn't seen much action in his day and he was anxious to take part in a fight.

"The way I was raised," Hefner said, "men die for cheatin'. Instead of stringin' you up, I'll put a bullet in your head. Anyone here object?"

"Shoot 'im!" Middles said again.

"I object," Clint said, and everyone looked at him. He was standing about ten feet from the scene.

"Who is that?" Hefner asked.

"It's Adams," Middles said.

"He'll leave town, Hefner," Clint said, "but not in a pine box. Put the gun down before you do something you'll regret."

Although he was still as mad as hell, Hefner was no cold-blooded killer. Nervously, his eyes flicked over toward Clint.

"Why you standin' up for him, Adams?" he asked.

"I'm not," Clint said. "I'm standing up for you, Dan. If you kill him, you'll have to pay."

"He was cheatin'."

Clint decided not to say that he knew that.

"Then he'll leave town and leave his money behind."

"I don't think—" Whiteoak started, but Clint silenced him.

"Shut up, Whiteoak!" He turned his attention back to Hefner. "Put the gun away, Dan."

"Shoot 'im!" Tom Middles shouted.

"Shut up!" Dan Hefner and Clint said at the same time.

Grudgingly, Hefner uncocked his gun and put it back in his holster.

"Thank you, Mr. Adams," Whiteoak said, getting shakily to his feet and brushing off his clothes, "but about the money—"

"Shut up and get out, Whiteoak, and leave the money."

"But—"

"You're lucky to get away with your life."

Whiteoak seemed to give the matter one last thought, then shrugged, brushed one last piece of sawdust off his jacket, and walked toward the door. Watching the entire scene Tom Middles's face turned a bright, angry red.

"He ain't walkin' out of here scot-free!" raged the young man.

Middles lunged for Whiteoak's back, pouncing on the older man, knocking them both to the floor. The pair rolled around on the ground as Whiteoak struggled to get free of Middles's grappling arms and legs. The boy was itching for a fight and wouldn't be denied it.

Clint was taken by surprise by Middles's sudden move. Wanting to defuse the entire situation before it got out of hand, he jumped into the brawl, trying to pull Middles away from Whiteoak. After a few seconds of dodging wild punches, Clint managed to pull the young man off the professor.

"C'mon, boy," Clint said, "don't get—"

Clint's words were cut off when he noticed Whiteoak, who, still on the floor, sat up and flicked his right arm outward. A two-shot derringer leapt forth into his hand. Before Whiteoak could aim the pistol, though, Clint released Middles and went for his own gun to keep Whiteoak from firing at the young man.

A shot echoed through the confines of the saloon, fired by neither Clint nor Whiteoak. Unnoticed by everyone, Dan Hefner had drawn his gun again and fired at Whiteoak. The slug took a chunk out of one of the other gaming tables behind Whiteoak, missing the con man by a mile. Before Hefner had a chance to take better aim, and before Whiteoak could retaliate, Clint fired his gun into the ceiling three quick times.

"Drop your guns!" he commanded loudly.

Tom Middles, pushed over the edge by the goings-on, reached behind his back for the .32 caliber revolver he kept there in his belt. Clint swung his own pistol quickly, smacking it into the back of the boy's head. Middles slumped to the floor. He'd have a bump on his head, but he'd be alive.

"Drop that derringer, Professor!" Clint said.

Whiteoak knew when he was outclassed. He let the little gun drop to the floor and then showed his empty hands.

"Hefner, drop it!"

Hefner made the same decision and dropped his gun.

"Now, don't anybody else draw a gun," Clint said, wondering where the hell the sheriff of this town was. "This incident is finished."

He walked over to Whiteoak and said, "You've caused enough trouble tonight, Professor. Let's go."

Clint walked Whiteoak out of the saloon and in the direction of his wagon.

THIRTEEN

Clint shoved Whiteoak down the street away from the Diamondback Saloon. The professor wasn't resisting, so Clint holstered his gun.

"Isn't it bad enough you bilk these people out of their money by selling them your bogus tonic?" Clint demanded. "You have to cheat them at cards, too?"

"A man's got to make a living."

"Maybe I should have let you get yourself out of that mess back there." Clint placed a hand on Whiteoak's shoulder and spun the man around. "You almost got yourself killed over a two-bit card game."

"It was a two-*dollar* card game—"

"It still wasn't worth getting killed over," Clint said, cutting the man off. "Professor, I suggest you hitch up your wagon and get the hell out of here before those people change their minds about shooting you. I don't even know why I saved your ass back there."

"You loved every minute of it."

"What?"

"We're the same, you and I, Adams. We like living life on the edge. I get my thrills by tricking people out of their money. It's dangerous work. You get your thrills by putting your life on the line for a friend."

"You're no friend of mine, Whiteoak. I'm no lying thief who needed his fat pulled out of the frying pan. And I don't go around looking for causes."

"Yeah?" Whiteoak asked. "Then why did you bother coming to the defense of a lying, two-bit thief like me?"

"Like I said inside, Whiteoak," Clint said, "I was trying to save them from shooting you. I did what I did to keep *anyone* from getting killed, and going to jail."

What the medicine man said next surprised Clint.

"Come with me, Adams."

"What?"

"We'd make one helluva team, you and I. I'll cut you in on the money and together we'll become rich men."

It was all Clint could do not to knock the man's teeth out. Suddenly, all of the liking he'd acquired for the man during the game faded away completely.

"Just get the hell away from me, Whiteoak," he said, waving his hand, as if swatting away a pesky fly. "I don't care where you go, just leave and don't come back here—and think about doing something else for a living."

"There's nothing so satisfying, Mr. Adams, as living life on the edge," Whiteoak said. "Tell me I'm wrong."

Clint just turned away from the man and started for his hotel. Henry Whiteoak seemed too far gone to save—and Clint wasn't in the business of saving men from themselves, anyway. He wanted nothing more to do with the man. Although he'd had an eventful few hours, the excitement wasn't worth the trouble that Whiteoak brought with him.

He made his way back to his hotel room, still feeling the pulse of adrenaline from the confrontations inside and outside of the Diamondback. Clint was ready for some rest. He wasn't sure if it was the wear and tear of the long day, or something else, but during his walk back to the hotel he had the feeling he was being followed.

Checking over his shoulder and listening for footsteps other than his own, Clint could find no one else on the quiet streets. Shaking off his suspicions he entered the hotel, climbed the stairs, and went to his room. Just as he removed his gun belt and boots, sat on the bed, and began to relax his muscles, a knock on his door shattered his brief moment of peace.

After he reached over and picked his gun up from the holster lying on the floor, Clint carefully approached the door, listening for a clue as to who was on the other side. Hearing nothing suspicious he opened the door a crack and peered outside.

"I didn't come too late," Marie Groder asked, "did I?"

"No," Clint said, feeling foolish. He put the gun behind his back and opened the door wide. "You didn't come late."

FOURTEEN

Marie Groder had changed into a different dress, one that was lower cut and tighter than the one she'd been wearing that afternoon. This time she didn't look half as sweet and innocent as before. However, when she stepped into the room she still appeared a bit timid. It was obvious she really didn't make a habit out of meeting with strange men.

Clint closed the door behind her, feeling more than a little foolish. Marie caught a glimpse of the gun behind his back and tensed at the sight of it.

"You *were* expecting me, weren't you?" she asked, somewhat apprehensively.

Clint put the gun back in its holster and hung it on the bedpost.

"I've just had a rather strange evening, and I didn't know what to expect."

"I heard what happened at the Diamondback," she said. "Are you all right?"

Clint stepped up close to her, stared into her rich, blue

eyes, and kissed her gently on the mouth. She was receptive to the advance. Her arms snaked around his back to hold him close to her own body.

"Do I feel all right to you?"

Letting her actions speak for her, Marie lifted her face to Clint's and kissed him again. This time she licked his lips and allowed his tongue to probe her mouth, as he tasted her sweet breath mingling with his own.

"Oh, Clint," she gasped. She held him tighter now, and Clint could feel the warmth of her body through the thin material of her summer dress.

Marie let him go and took a few steps back from him. After reaching around to unfasten her dress, she allowed the garment to fall to the floor and stood naked in front of him. Her body was smooth and firm in all the right places. Firm, rounded breasts heaved with every breath as passion overtook her. Curving thighs tapered into muscular legs, with a patch of wild blond hair between her legs.

Marie walked over to the bed while Clint undressed. When she lay down on the bed her eyes took in the sight of Clint's body, hard and ready for her.

Clint knelt by the side of the bed and kissed her belly, surprising her. She wrapped her fingers in his hair as he poked her navel with his tongue, then kissed his way up to her breasts. He nibbled her breasts gently, then took each of her hard nipples into his mouth and sucked them in turn.

She gasped and reached for him to pull him onto the bed with her. When he was lying beside her she slid her hand down between his legs, and he did the same. He found her hot and wet and stroked her until she was even wetter. She swayed her hips back and forth, adding to the movement of his fingers.

"Oh, God," she moaned, "like that, yes . . ."

Soon Clint had his face between her legs and was tasting the tender flesh there. With eager hands Marie reached down to spread herself even wider for him, allowing him to enter her with his tongue.

"Mmm, Clint, oh, yes . . ." she breathed.

Clint couldn't hold off any longer. His own need was growing too great. He climbed atop her as she grabbed at his buttocks and pulled him into her. His hard shaft plunged deeply into her, and she let out a joyous squeal as she felt him inside of her. After a few long, slow strokes she began to buck frantically beneath him, driving him to a faster, harder pace.

She clung to him as though her life depended on it as he drove into her again and again. Clint mentally cursed the feeling that soon welled up inside of him. He could feel that he was going to burst any second and he didn't want this to ever end. With Marie's soft, warm body under him, clinging to him, he wished he could ride her forever.

Just as Marie let out a groan from deep in the back of her throat as she seemed to tighten around his cock, Clint let out a great groan of his own as he emptied into her.

Immediately afterwards both of them just lay there in each other's arms, with him still on top of her and inside of her. At that moment neither of them could have moved if they wanted to.

"Oh, Clint . . . that was . . . that was . . ."

She was apparently too breathless to finish, so he did it for her.

"Yes," he agreed, "it was. . . ."

As she tried to catch her breath, Clint felt her strong

thighs brushing up against his sides and her tight body squirming under his weight. The motions aroused him again and he began to move inside of her.

"Oh, no, you don't," she said.

With a strength he wouldn't have thought she had, Marie pushed him off of her and onto his back. Before he knew it, she was on top of him, straddling him and impaling herself on him.

"It's my turn to ride," she said, a wicked, lustful look on her beautiful face.

No, Clint thought as Marie rocked on top of him, she certainly wasn't the innocent little small-town girl he'd thought she was.

FIFTEEN

Because Running Water, Oklahoma, was such a small town the gambling life was winding down by the hour of two in the morning. In his life Sage Johnson had been in two-day long poker games with only an occasional walk to wake himself up. That was in much bigger towns . . . wilder towns. Although Johnson was getting comfortable in Running Water, he could never call the place big or wild.

All in all, even with the early stopping time, Johnson had made some decent money during the night. After he paid the house its share, he left the Royal Lady saloon with a smile on his face. As he walked out to the deserted street it was nearly three. He heard a sound from a nearby alley.

He squinted into the darkness, trying to make out the source of the noise.

''Anyone there?''

A lanky man in a worn duster stepped out from the alley, his head bowed, allowing his hat to cover his face.

Another man came out behind him with his hands balled into fists, hanging loosely at his sides. The man in the duster reached under the long coat as he looked up into Johnson's eyes. Immediately, Sage Johnson recognized him.

"Oh, shit," he said, groping for his Colt.

He knew the man's face, so he knew why he was there and who would be with him. It was because of these men that Johnson was laying low and staying away from bigger towns—but they had found him anyway.

As Johnson's hand found the butt of his revolver, Luke Kylie had his shotgun out and pointed at him. Jeremiah Weller still approached Johnson, not seeming to care that the man had his hand on his gun.

"You know why we're here, Johnson," Kylie said. "If you don't want to die right now, you best throw your hands up and hear me out."

Johnson, his hand gripping his pistol now, squinted at the two figures and past them, looking for the third man. He knew that if the third man wasn't there he had a fighting chance to leave Running Water alive.

"Where's Duggin?" he asked.

"You got bigger worries than him, Sage," Kylie said. "Mr. Halsey doesn't want you. He wants Whiteoak. Now, you tell us where he's at, along with the other fellas you worked with, and we'll let you go."

Johnson looked at Weller, who now stood within arm's reach. After he'd worked with Whiteoak to con Joe Halsey all the men went their separate ways, running from the assassins they knew Halsey would send after them. Although Johnson knew where some of those boys were, he had no clue as to where Whiteoak was. Looking back he realized that Whiteoak was the only one who had kept his hiding place a secret. Now he knew why.

Johnson's face went dark. Seeing only the two men in front of him he thought he might have a chance to take them down. One had no gun in his hands, while the other was holding a shotgun.

Not wanting to die or betray his friends Johnson made his decision. His arm muscles tensed as he tightened his grip on his Colt. As he started to draw the weapon to make his play, he felt something cold and hard against the back of his head, behind his left ear. A metallic click soon followed, freezing him in mid-draw.

"Now, Sage," said the man who was holding a .45 to the back of Johnson's head, "that's no way to treat some friendly faces from your past."

"Duggin," Johnson said, his voice a whisper as fear of the man caused his mouth to go dry.

"Move your hand away from your gun, Sage . . . that's it." Duggin removed the gun from its holster and tossed it aside. "Now you come along with us, Sage. We got some questions for you. And in case you decide to run away on us again . . ."

Johnson felt the barrel of Duggin's second gun digging into his body. This time, instead of behind his head the barrel was buried in the calf of his right leg. He realized what was about to happen just before his body erupted with fiery pain as Duggin blew a hole through his leg.

The sound of the shot was muffled by the point-blank range, but just to be safe Kylie and Weller rushed over and grabbed the wounded man, carrying him off quickly to a nearby stable where they could finish their business in private.

Duggin checked up and down the street before holstering his weapons. He looked down at Johnson's blood and dipped his toe in it before following the others into the stable.

In the stable four of the five stalls were occupied. Weller and Kylie took Johnson into the fifth stall and dropped him to the ground. Kylie knelt next to Johnson and kept his hand over his mouth, muffling the man's cries of pain.

Weller removed his bowie knife from its leather sheath as John Duggin strolled into the stable.

"If you can't keep quiet, Sage . . ." Weller said, holding the blade over the man's fresh leg wound, "I'll bury this here knife in your leg and give you something to really scream about."

John Duggin made his way to the stall where his men had Sage Johnson. He calmly walked over to the fallen man and knelt down by him, across from Kylie. Duggin could see that his men were ready to counter any move Johnson might make, but seeing the fear in the man's eyes he was sure that Sage Johnson was all out of heroic moves.

"Now, Sage," Duggin said, "I just want you to tell me what I want to know. Mr. Halsey is very upset with you and your friends. I had to at least wound you to keep him happy."

Duggin looked up and winked at Kylie.

"If you tell me where your swindling partners are, I won't have to shoot you again," the Killer continued. "We'll just say you escaped."

Duggin smiled and spoke to the other two assassins. "Ain't that right, boys?"

"Sure," Kylie said, and Weller just nodded.

"You see, Sage?" Duggin said. "You just have to tell us what we want to know and we'll be on our way."

SIXTEEN

Although Johnson didn't want to hand his friends over to these killers, he was sure that it was his only chance at survival.

Johnson blinked the sweat from his eyes as he looked up at Duggin.

"Kylie's gonna take his hand away from your mouth, Sage," Duggin said. "Just tell us where we can find somebody."

Tired of waiting, Weller began pressing the blade of his knife against Johnson's wound as the other man removed his hand. Each little stab sent a burning agony through Johnson's whole body.

"Brazzleton," he croaked.

"What's that, Sage?" Duggin asked. He spoke with a velvet tongue as he produced his pistols from beneath his coat.

"Andy Crawford and Dwight Dixon," Johnson said. "They were the ones who fixed up the fake deeds and papers for the land Halsey bought. Those two are in

Brazzleton. It's a town on the Texas and Oklahoma border.''

Johnson figured there was no harm in telling Duggin this. When the man spared his life and left, he could contact Crawford and Dixon and warn them.

Duggin cocked one of his .45's and shoved the barrel in Johnson's mouth.

"How do I know you're not lying to protect your piece of shit hide?"

Panicking, Johnson tried to babble something to assure the Killer he was telling the truth, but his words were garbled by the cold steel in his mouth. While the man tried to form audible words, Duggin nodded to Weller, whose knife was still poised over Johnson's wounded leg.

When Johnson saw Weller's muscles tense and his grip tighten on the handle of the bowie knife, the man's babbling instantly stopped. A split second later the blade tore through the bloody tunnel carved by Duggin's bullet and came out the other side on the hard-packed dirt floor of the stable. Johnson's teeth clamped down on the barrel of Duggin's revolver as an agonized moan rumbled from the back of his throat.

When Duggin saw the victim actually bite on the end of his gun, he didn't even try to suppress the smile from crossing his face. He even started to laugh as he pulled the trigger, blowing out the back of Johnson's head.

Luke Kylie went outside to see if they'd attracted any attention, and then knocked on the stable door when he returned with their horses.

"All clear," he said.

For a minute John Duggin stared at the grimace on Johnson's dead face. A giddy chuckle shook his body as he wiped the blood from his .45. He noticed some bloodstains on his coat as he was climbing into his saddle.

As the assassins rode into the night, leaving Running Water behind, Duggin decided not to clean the grim trademark from his clothing. He would leave the blood on his jacket for a while . . . at least until they got to Brazzleton.

SEVENTEEN

When morning came to Wider's Canyon the sunlight pierced through Clint Adams's sleep and opened his eyes to the supple form of Marie Groder lying beside him. She was already awake and looking at him.

"You're lazy," she said.

"You wore me out last night."

"I've been waiting for you to wake up," she said. "I'm hungry."

Clint swung his legs over the side of the bed, stretched his arms, and walked over to the window. Looking out, his good mood was broken by the sight of the ragged, dreary scenery.

Marie slipped from the covers and came up behind him, sliding her arms around his waist and pressing her breasts against his back.

"It's not a pretty sight in the morning, is it?" she asked.

"No."

"Actually, it's not a pretty sight at any time."

For a moment he thought she might ask to go with him when he left, but then the moment passed.

"We better get dressed and have some breakfast," he said.

She started to dress and he took special pleasure in watching her, then dressed himself.

"How about a nice big breakfast, huh?" she asked.

"Sounds good to me."

Marie wrapped her arms around Clint's waist again, this time from the front, and looked into his eyes. The soft moment made what Clint had to say even more difficult. He'd been through the same thing before many times and it was never easy, especially with someone as nice and as special as Marie Groder.

"I, uh . . ." he said, looking for the right words.

"Well, what is it?" she asked.

"I'm hungry," he said. "Let's go eat."

Marie and Clint had breakfast at Jarvis's. On the way Clint saw that Whiteoak's wagon was still on the street. If he had to spend one more day in town with Whiteoak . . .

"He's going to get himself killed if he stays," Marie observed.

"That's his problem," Clint said harshly.

Clint had an average steak and runny eggs while Marie had biscuits and gravy. When the opportunity presented itself, Clint decided to tell Marie his plans for the day.

"Marie, I hate to tell you this, but . . ."

She held up a hand to keep him from saying any more.

"You're leaving town today."

"Yes, but it's not . . ."

She stopped him again.

"You don't have to explain anything to me, Clint. I usually don't move this fast on men who I like, but I knew you wouldn't be here for very long. When are you leaving?"

"Today," he said, "right after breakfast. I don't want to run into Whiteoak again."

"I understand."

"I never intended to stop here . . ."

"I understand," she said again, "really."

The rest of the meal was finished in silence. Marie walked with Clint to his hotel so he could collect his gear. In front of the building she wrapped her arms around him and kissed him, not caring who saw.

"You will remember to come and see me when you're in these parts again, won't you?" she asked.

"You know I will."

Clint held her tight and kissed her again. It was a long, passionate kiss that would be their final good-bye. He had no idea if he would ever see her again. Most of the time his travels took control of him, rather than the other way around.

The main thing that was on his mind now was to put as much distance between himself and Henry Whiteoak as possible. He knew that the man was bad news, pure and simple.

After one final look, Marie turned and headed back to her home and normal life. Clint went up to his room, collected his things, and checked out of the hotel. He walked directly to the livery, saddled Duke, settled his bill, and rode out of town.

He wanted to get back on the open range, back to his original plan of just riding aimlessly wherever the big black gelding took him. He knew some friends he could visit who didn't live too far away, but he thought he'd save that for the trip back.

Sitting astride the big black gelding, he quickly regained the spirit he'd had before the stopover in Wider's Canyon. It was just him and Duke, riding for no better reason than to ride. By the time Wider's Canyon was a speck on the horizon, he was fully relaxed again.

This, he thought, is more like it.

Henry Whiteoak had seen Clint Adams walking to the livery and knew he was leaving town. He, himself, would also be leaving town soon. It was a course of action suggested to him by Clint and then, this morning, by the sheriff, who had been so conspicuously absent last night.

As he watched Clint Adams walk to the livery he got an idea. He saw a newer, better course of action than he had seen before.

What, he asked himself, did he need more than anything else right now? Who had been there to pull his fat out of the fire when his life depend on it? Hurriedly, he went to the livery and found a boy working there. He took fifty cents from his pocket.

"Would you like to have this?" he asked the boy, who was in his early teens.

"Sure!"

"A man just got on a horse and rode out of here. You know the one I mean?"

"Yes, sir," the boy said. "It was a beautiful, big black gelding."

"That's the one," Whiteoak said. "Do you know where he and his master are off to?"

"No, sir," the boy said, looking at the money worriedly now, "he didn't say."

Whiteoak leaned closer to the boy.

"Do you know which way they headed when they left town?"

With renewed hope of getting Whiteoak's money, the boy's face lit up and he eagerly nodded his head.

A half hour later Henry Whiteoak was guiding his wagon out of town, heading in the same direction as Clint Adams.

EIGHTEEN

The border town of Brazzleton, sitting on the edge of Texas and Oklahoma, was new and bustling with people. Most of the credit for its recent popularity was given to the outlaws and bandits who found more than a few benefits to living a few minutes away from another state. Men on the run from either side could easily hop over to the other if they had to make themselves scarce.

The buildings looked clean and new, which was more than could be said for most of the people occupying them. Many of the saloons and houses of ill repute were so new and had their management change hands so many times that few of them even had names. On the main street two saloons sat side by side and were simply called Saloon #1 and Saloon #2.

Even though the saloons had no names and the whore-houses were known mainly by reputation, none of the residents seemed to mind. Most of them probably wouldn't be staying too long anyway. A sharp contrast to the quiet family atmosphere of Wider's Canyon, Brazzleton was always loud and teeming with life.

The night John Duggin rode into town with Weller and Kylie was like any other. The air was alive with the sounds of raised voices, piano music, and gunfire, none of which diverted the killers' attention from their grim purpose. Their eyes carefully scanned the groups of men gathered around the gaming halls, looking for the two faces that belonged to Andy Crawford and Dwight Dixon.

Duggin scowled under the trail dust that coated his face. Just by looking at the rowdy town and its inhabitants, he knew it was going to be harder to locate the two men amid the turmoil than it had been to find Sage Johnson. On the other hand, with all that the town had to offer, Duggin was sure that the time spent there wouldn't be so bad.

Duggin had known Sage Johnson for the small-timer that he was. He also knew Andy Crawford on sight, because Crawford used to be one of Joe Halsey's land scouts. Henry Whiteoak must have offered Crawford a big cut to get him to cross Joe Halsey.

As for Dwight Dixon, Duggin had a description of the man to go by, and that was all.

The Killer looked over at his men, riding on either side of him. Weller and Kylie would never complain, but he knew they had to be tired of riding and working for the past few weeks without rest.

"Okay, boys," Duggin said as he reined his horse to a stop in front of the livery stable. "Let's drop the horses here and get a place to stay. I know you two are ready to go to work, but I think I'll take some time to scout out the town. Why don't you fellas scout out that place."

He pointed to a two-story building that had a steady stream of traffic going in and out of it. Leaning out the second-floor windows were women of all shapes and sizes, calling to the passing men, raising their skirts, lowering their blouses, showing off what they had.

Without a word of protest, Weller and Kylie dropped from their mounts and removed their saddlebags and rifles. After the animals were put up in the stable and the men had stored their gear in a cheap hotel room, Weller and Kylie headed straight back to the whorehouse, while Duggin strode to the source of most of the town's commotion.

A long row of gambling houses, saloons, and brothels lined both sides of the street. Duggin shook his head, thinking about the chore that it would be to find two needles in this haystack. Looking around, all the dirty, drunken faces started to look the same.

By the time he found a saloon to his liking and got a few drinks in him, Duggin decided he was just too tired to continue hunting tonight. He decided to have a couple more drinks, join his men back at the brothel, and get a warm bed and a warm woman to spend the night with.

After all, tomorrow was another day.

NINETEEN

Clint Adams had been riding alone and sleeping in open country for three days after Wider's Canyon when he began to run low on supplies. In his hurry to get out of Wider's Canyon, he had neglected to stock up on the essentials. With the combination of being diverted from his plans, getting in a bar fight, and being propositioned by Henry Whiteoak, Clint had just wanted to get away from the whole situation. Now he wanted to find a place to stock up.

Looking back, with the last few days of quiet relaxation behind him, he saw how he had allowed the medicine man to get under his skin. Lulled by the man's flamboyance, by his facade, it took a while to see what he really was. His idea of living on the edge was not the same as Clint's. Bilking people and cheating people out of their money was not Clint's idea of living life to its fullest.

By the time Clint reined Duke to a halt in a spot next to a small, trickling brook, the sun was turning to the dusky red that signaled the end of another day. Clint filled his lungs with clean Texas air.

After removing the saddle from Duke's back and making camp, he sat down next to his fire and started preparing the last of his food. Dinner was bacon, beef jerky, and coffee . . . again.

He knew the lay of the land well enough to know that the nearest town for him to head for to stock up on supplies was about half a day's ride northwest.

Thinking about riding to town Clint's body started craving the luxuries of indoor living. He'd had no such cravings when he stopped in Wider's Canyon. He decided this time that he'd spend the next few days eating hot, home-cooked meals and sleeping in a real bed. He recalled from his last visit to the town of Fort Wagner that he'd have no trouble finding someone to spend some time with.

Fort Wagner was a booming town with more than its share of saloons and gaming halls. With that combination Clint had no doubt that he'd be able to keep himself busy for a while—and this time his stop in a town was by his own choice. He had to admit that the little taste of poker he'd had in Wider's Canyon, although he had not enjoyed it, had whetted his appetite for it a bit.

Clint ate the rest of his meager meal and fixed himself some more coffee. Coffee was the one thing he always had an overabundance of. But a man couldn't live by coffee alone.

Later he settled himself on his back with his head on his rolled up blanket, stared at the stars, and soon drifted off to sleep.

It was late afternoon by the time Clint rode into the town of Fort Wagner. By that time the place was already alive and kicking, surging with life.

The oldest buildings were on the other side of town and they consisted mainly of dry goods stores and homes. The newer buildings were the telegraph office, a fancy hotel, and one of the saloons that had opened up a week before Clint's arrival. Fort Wagner was easily triple the size of Wider's Canyon and seemed about ready to burst with the people who were wandering the streets and stuffing the dance halls and saloons.

Clint was impressed with the change in the town since his last visit. The town had grown faster than most and had apparently become rowdier than he remembered. People were milling about no matter where he looked. Most of them walked in groups of three, four, or more, and he wondered if this was for protection. However, the few loners he spotted looked very capable of handling themselves. Even at this relatively early hour men were still calling and shouting to one another drunkenly, and staggering in and out of saloons with liquor bottles in their hands.

Clint passed the sheriff's office on his way to the livery and decided to check in with the local law after putting Duke up for the night and before showing himself in the town's saloons and gambling halls. With a town this size he knew he'd be recognized eventually, and he preferred to have the law already on his side.

When he dropped Duke off at the livery he took the stable boy aside and held a dollar out to him.

"I want you to take good care of him," he told the boy, who appeared to be all of thirteen. "Make sure no one comes around him except me."

"Yes, sir," the boy said, snatching the money. "Don't worry. We ain't had trouble with horse thieves since the last hangin'. We strung three of them up at once. Everybody's too busy with the tournament to worry about stealin' horses anyway.''

''Tournament? What tournament is that?''

''Ain't that why you're here . . . for the big poker tournament?''

Clint shook his head and smiled. That answered some of his questions about the change in the town. A poker tournament could bring a lot of people to one place. Unfortunately, it often brought the wrong kind of people.

''Maybe I'll look into it,'' Clint told the kid. He grabbed his saddlebags and rifle.

''Mister, you got a place to stay?''

''No, but I figured I'd just check with the nearest hotel.''

''That'd be the Texas Grand. Got the softest beds in town and it's brand-new. Miss Downing opened it a month ago.''

''Well, then, maybe you better give me directions to the Texas Grand, boy,'' Clint said.

''I hope they got some rooms left,'' the kid said, and gave Clint the directions he needed.

''I hope so, too,'' Clint said. The idea of staying in a brand-new hotel appealed to him. ''See ya.''

TWENTY

As Clint left the livery he could feel the excitement in the air before he walked ten feet. As he drew nearer the saloon district he could hear tinny pianos dueling from different establishments and rowdy fistfights going on, all within one block.

The sheriff's office was a small shack sitting in the shadow of a newer, much larger building at the end of the street. Compared to the rest of the town the tiny office seemed deserted. Clint had the feeling that the law might have simply given up on the place.

He knocked on the door, then knocked again. After a few more raps the door was opened by a stout, muscular man in his late thirties, wearing faded jeans, a white shirt, and a black vest with a silver star pinned to it. The man looked just as tired and worn-out as Clint would have expected the sheriff of such a wild town to be.

"Can I do somethin' for ya?" the sheriff asked.

"Evening, Sheriff," Clint said, walking past the man into the office. "I just got to town and this place sure isn't anything like I remembered it being last year.''

"A lot's changed in a year.''

The sheriff closed the door, walked to his desk, and sat down behind it.

"What can I do for you?''

"My name is Clint Adams. I just thought I'd check in with you and let you know I'm here.''

"Sure,'' the lawman said, "I know who you are. You know, I've been needing some help around here, but I never expected this.''

"What? Now hold on—''

The sheriff opened a drawer, pulled out a deputy's badge, and tossed it on the desk.

"Say the word and you're hired.''

"Now hold on, Sheriff,'' Clint said again. "I didn't come here to be deputized.''

The man looked disappointed.

"What did you come here for then, Adams?''

"I was just stopping by for one night and I heard about the tournament.''

"That damn tournament!'' the man spat. "It's brought every lowlife from miles around into town.''

"Then why do you let it go on?''

The sheriff laughed without humor.

"I got no choice in the matter, Adams,'' he said. "The mayor is behind it.''

"Who's the mayor?''

"I don't even know,'' the lawman said.

"What's that mean?''

"It means they just had an election and I ain't even checked to see who won yet.''

"Then how do you know he's behind the tournament?''

"Because both of the men who were runnin' are gamblers,'' the man said. "It don't matter who won."

"If you don't like it," Clint said, "why don't you just quit?"

"Because I ain't a quitter," the sheriff said. "Besides, what would I do then? Play poker?"

"Is this town the way it is because of the tournament?"

The man shook his head, then added, "But the tournament sure crowns it off, don't it? This place has been gettin' worse and worse, and now this damned tournament. After this there'll be nothin' but gamblers hereabouts—gamblers, thieves, and murderers. They all go hand in hand."

Clint didn't exactly agree, but he kept his notions to himself.

"Don't you have any deputies at all?"

"None," the man said. "I sent for some help days ago, but nobody's come yet."

"Well, I'm sorry, but I'm just not disposed to putting a badge on."

"That's okay," the man said. "Nobody is."

"I'll buy you a drink, though."

"That's kind of you. I'll be out on patrol soon. I'll keep an eye out for you. By the way, my name's Oldman, Harve Oldman."

Anxious to find the hotel and get settled in, Clint left Sheriff Oldman to his problems and continued to follow the directions given him by the boy. Oddly, they seemed to be taking him away from the rowdy district of town.

Finally, he came to the Texas Grand, and while he could still hear the commotion behind him, it wasn't really in the same part of town as the saloons and gambling halls—which suited him just fine.

TWENTY-ONE

Jeremiah Weller entered the huge, open room that made up Brazzleton's Saloon #2. As always the place was full of life with four poker tables going, all of them full. Looking around at the various men and women populating the place, Weller felt that he truly belonged here.

It had only been eight months since he started working with John "The Killer" Duggin and Luke Kylie. Before that he'd spent his life on the run, hiding out in places very much like Brazzleton. Now he had more money put away then he'd ever seen in his life, and all because John Duggin had recognized the value of Weller's innate violent tendencies.

Ever since he was a kid Weller had been a violent person. Working with Duggin and getting paid to beat the hell out of people was truly Weller's dream job.

The big man strode up to the bar and ordered a whiskey. When the drink came, Weller scanned the saloon for the faces he'd memorized last night, when the three assassins had split up to search for their prey. They'd decided to cover the whole town, piece by piece.

He was searching the saloons and nearby brothels. Luke Kylie would be looking at the gaming halls and hotels, while Duggin himself would be looking everywhere else.

Weller wasn't quite sure what Duggin had meant when he'd told him that—he'd be looking "everywhere else"—but he had learned long ago not to question Duggin. After all, the man who'd had his job before him had been shot for asking too many questions.

Anyway, he was happy with his assignment of blending into the saloon crowd and keeping an eye out for the faces of Andy Crawford and Dwight Dixon. Actually, they knew what Crawford looked like. Dixon was another story, but they hoped that when they found Crawford, Dixon would be right there next to him.

Weller snatched his drink from the bar and walked over to the poker tables. He scanned all of the faces there and didn't find a match for Crawford's, or for the description they had of Dixon's. He didn't put much faith in the description, though. Hell, except for a point or two, it could have matched him.

He decided to blend in by sitting in on a few hands of poker or finding a chair at a table and keeping an eye on the door. Saloon #2 was the largest in town. Sooner or later, he figured, everybody came in there.

Two hours later he still hadn't seen anybody. He decided that he'd spent enough time at Saloon #2 and he left and headed for Saloon #1.

I love my job, he thought.

"Excuse me, sir . . . wrong room."

The scrawny hotel clerk stood aside, let the man

standing next to him gaze into the room, apologized one more time, and closed the door.

If it wasn't for the shotgun under the man's duster, the clerk would not have been bothering his guests this way.

The man standing next to him was not a man to be refused, however. The clerk could tell by looking at Luke Kylie that the man was a killer. He knew that his life was in danger and the only way to save it was to do what the man told him to do, which was show him every room in the hotel—and that's just what he was doing.

The door the clerk had just hastily closed was the last one. He hoped now that the man with the shotgun would leave. To his everlasting relief the man asked for directions to the next hotel. The clerk happily complied and Luke Kylie left, leaving the clerk so weak in the knees with relief that he slumped to the floor.

When Luke arrived at Martha's Boardinghouse, where the other clerk had sent him, the woman standing behind the desk asked, "How can I help you?"

Without answering Kylie grabbed the register and turned it around so he could read it. He scanned it for Crawford's or Dixon's name. Not finding them he looked at the woman, a robust redhead in her early forties. She had lived long enough to know when to speak and when not to speak. She waited for the man to say what he wanted.

"You can help me by shutting the hell up, grabbing those keys, and letting me into every room you've rented in this dump."

"Can you give me a good reason?" she asked calmly.

In spite of himself Kylie found himself liking the

woman. He moved his coat aside and showed her his shotgun.

"Is this reason enough?"

"I'll get my skeleton key," she said. "It opens every room in the place."

"Smart lady."

She grabbed her skeleton key off the hook on the wall and held it out to him.

"Oh, no," he said, "I want you to come with me. I like your company."

Lucky me, the woman thought, but wisely she continued to remain silent. She came out from behind the desk and led Kylie up the stairs.

Kylie sighed to himself as he thought about spending the rest of the night doing this. He was hoping to find the men in one of the rooms, where they would put up a fight, allowing him to go against orders and gun them down.

If the hotels led to a dead end he'd get to search all the gaming halls. At least that way he could get a drink.

John Duggin walked the back streets of Brazzleton, looking for his prey. He was confident that his men would do their best to find the two targets while covering the more populated parts of town. He, on the other hand, would search through the side streets, back streets, and alleys, and stretches of homes and stores. He was completely at home on the dark, dirty, deserted streets.

Duggin thought of himself as a hunter. He enjoyed the chase almost as much as making the kill. Well, maybe he enjoyed the kill just a little bit more. As he patrolled, he reached out with his senses and let his instincts take over. Like a drunk who, even when he was on the verge of passing out, knew where his bottle was,

Duggin thought he might be able to find Andy Crawford and Dwight Dixon by using his specially tuned perception.

Although his hunter's instincts were not helping him much at the moment, he knew he wouldn't be leaving this town without the scalps of these men hanging from his belt—figuratively speaking, of course.

He grinned in the darkness of the alley at the thought of actually scalping someone.

With the bloody images running through his mind, Duggin quickened his pace, searching for the two doomed men almost anxiously. More than anything the Killer wanted to find them and show them just how painful dying could really be.

He'd make them beg for death.

TWENTY-TWO

The Texas Grand Hotel was the most ornate building in the entire town of Fort Wagner. The sign on the front of the structure displayed the name in dark green flowing letters, inviting those with the finests tastes to enjoy its hospitality. Compared to the rest of the wild town, the hotel was like a calm resting place in the middle of a raging storm.

Clint Adams had no trouble finding the place and only needed to use the first half of the directions he was given. It was so big he could see it from two blocks away. As he walked through the front doors, he was confident he'd made the right choice in staying here.

The lobby was open and clean, which was a nice change from the standard dirty rooms in most of the places he stayed throughout the West. When he saw the clerk standing behind the desk, his feelings about the place became even better.

She was tall, in her early thirties, had a soft, slender build, and a mane of black hair flowing over her shoulders. As he approached her he could smell the perfume she wore and could see the purple ribbons that were woven through her hair. She had no trouble fitting in with her beautiful surroundings.

"Hello, sir. Welcome to the Texas Grand."

Clint suddenly became painfully aware of his own appearance. Still fresh from the trail, he was covered with gritty dust from head to toe. When she extended her hand to him in greeting, he shrugged and shook his head.

"The last thing I'd want to do," he said, "is get you dirty. You're too beautiful for that."

She smiled and looked him straight in the eye. He liked that. Most women would have played coy, or been actually embarrassed.

"Maybe later, then," she said. "Would you like a room? We have quite a few available."

"With a place like this," he said, "I'm surprised you're not booked up—especially with this tournament in town."

"Most of the men in town for the tournament are saving their money for that," she said. "When I first opened this place I had plenty of business, but the complexion of this town has changed drastically from what it once seemed it would be. Lately the kind of people we get in town don't have the money or the inclination to stay someplace that's not a saloon or a brothel."

Clint looked around and noticed that while the hotel had a dining room, it didn't have a bar, as most hotels did.

"Having second thoughts?" she asked.

"No, ma'am," he said. "I'll take that room now."

"Good. Please sign in."

"Are you the owner?" he asked as he did so.

"Yes," she said. "My name is Katherine Downing.

Since you're the first man to come here who isn't drunk or trying to shoot up the place, I'll give you the Presidential Suite at the regular room rate.''

"That's very nice of you."

"It has a bathtub," she said. "If you'd like it filled, just let me know and I'll have it taken care of."

"I'd like that just fine."

She turned the register around to read his name. If she recognized it she gave no indication.

"Enjoy your stay, Mr. Adams."

After she gave Clint his key, he picked up his gear and paused before climbing the stairs to room 304.

"Will you be getting off work soon, Miss Downing?" he asked.

"In about two hours, Mr. Adams. Why?"

"Well, this town has changed quite a bit since the last time I was here, as you indicated. I could use a guide to find my way around."

She hesitated.

"Besides," he added, "once I've cleaned up I'd like to take you up on that handshake."

The tall brunette smiled, making her eyes sparkle.

"I'd like that very much, Mr. Adams."

"Good," he said, "I'll come back down in two hours. Perhaps you'll even let me buy you dinner. I'd like to sample your dining room."

"I think you'll find it to your liking."

"I'm sure I will."

Just like the rest of the hotel his suite was decorated like a palace. The furniture was clean and luxurious. Thick carpets covered the floor and expensive paintings lined the walls. Compared to the cheap hotel in Wider's Canyon and the outdoor living he'd been doing recently, he felt as if he'd died and gone to paradise.

Of course, it *was* the Presidential Suite.

Katherine Downing didn't seem to belong in the rowdy town of Fort Wagner. He pictured her in a different setting, like San Francisco or Denver. Then again, he was glad she was in Texas on this particular night, or he wouldn't be seeing her later.

There was a knock on the door, and he admitted the bellboy with the water for his bath.

TWENTY-THREE

After he was bathed, rested, and freshly dressed, Clint went back downstairs to meet with Katherine Downing. She was waiting for him, wearing a simple black cotton dress that showed off her smooth, trim body. She was carrying a shawl in one of her hands. Even with her black hair tied back she still seemed regal, much too good for this town.

And maybe for him.

"I hope I didn't keep you waiting too long," he said.

"It was worth the wait," she said. "You clean up quite nicely."

"Thank you."

She stuck out her hand without preamble and he took it. She had a nice firm handshake.

"Now that we've gotten that out of the way," she said, "let's eat."

She led him into the dining room, which was spacious with a high ceiling. Several of the tables were occupied, but for the most part the place was empty.

He followed her to a table at the back of the room, and immediately a waiter appeared.

"Good evening, boss," he said to her. He was short, balding, and apparently quite smitten with his "boss." It was obvious in the way he looked at her.

"I've asked you not to call me that, Tom."

"Sorry, bos—I mean, sorry. What will you and your guest be eating?"

She looked across the table at Clint and said, "May I?"

"Please."

She ordered for both of them, starting with chicken soup and then a roast chicken dinner.

"I hope you like chicken."

"I do."

"I love it, and since I own the hotel, there's a lot of it on the menu."

"I'm sure I'll enjoy it."

"Are you going to sign up for the tournament while you're here, Mr. Adams?"

"Please call me Clint."

"All right."

"I really wasn't thinking about getting into the tournament. Some of them have been known to go on for days, and I don't know if I want to be here that long."

"Is it a game you're familiar with?"

"Quite familiar, yes," he said, thinking about a tournament in Denver several months back that had some obvious differences with this one.

"But you're not a professional gambler?"

"No, I am not. What are the stakes, by the way?"

"From the gamblers who have entered in the past I understand the winnings can be fairly high each night.

Whoever ends up winning the most by the end of the tournament gets an extra three thousand dollars.''

"Not bad," he said, although he'd played in games where three thousand wouldn't have been enough to buy in.

Their dinner arrived, and they ate and passed the time with small talk until they were both done.

"That was very good, Katherine," he said, wiping his mouth with a cloth napkin. "Really fine."

"Thank you," she said, obviously quite pleased.

He looked around and said, "Why do I have the feeling that you have even more rooms available than you indicated?"

She looked away from his stare.

"Yes, it's true. I'm really not doing that well at all. That's why I was thinking of . . ."

"Of what?"

She looked at him.

"Of entering the tournament."

"Do you play poker?"

"Not very well, I'm afraid," she said, "but I could certainly use that three thousand dollars."

Clint doubted that she'd have much of a chance at the prize.

"I have a proposition for you, Clint."

"What's that, Katherine?"

She leaned forward and the look on her face was far from sexy. It was more businesslike.

"If you would play in the tournament for me, I'd back you."

"You mean I'd play with your money?"

"That's right."

"And what would be in it for me?"

"You'd keep whatever you won."

"And the three thousand?"

"That would be mine," she said. "That money would enable me to keep the hotel going until business picks up."

Clint didn't answer right away.

"What do you say?"

"I don't know, Katherine—"

"I'll throw in your room for free, as long as you're here."

He thought about it. Did he want to play poker for days in what sounded like a second-rate tournament? Did he want to stay in Fort Wagner for a few days longer than he'd planned?

Well, that might depend on the woman sitting across from him.

"I'll do it on one condition."

She sat back and eyed him suspiciously.

"What's that?"

"That you dine with me here, each evening."

"Is that all?" she asked, still suspicious. "Just dine?"

"Well," he said, "that's all I'm demanding. I guess we'd just have to see what else happened. What do you say?"

Now she took a moment to think about it, but only a moment.

"All right," she said, "done. Let's go." She got up from her chair.

"Where?"

"Over to the saloon where they're signing up," she said. "The tournament starts tonight."

"Tonight?"

She nodded and said, "In fact, in an hour."

"Looks like I got to town just in time," he said, following her out.

"I sure hope so," she said over her shoulder.

TWENTY-FOUR

She led him back into the noisy part of town and to a large saloon called the Red Hand Saloon. Over the door, on a piece of wooden plank, was painted a red hand. Clever.

When they entered, Clint was surprised the building hadn't burst. Everywhere he looked people were jammed in close together drinking, talking, or fighting.

Toward the back he could see empty tables that were roped off for the tournament. In the center of each table was a chip carousel and some decks of cards.

"How are they running this game?" he asked her.

"What do you mean?"

"Who deals?"

"The house."

He nodded. At least he wouldn't have to contend with a different dealer each hand.

As Clint looked around he saw that every man in the place was armed. He wondered if weapons would be allowed at the poker tables. If they were, then it was no wonder Sheriff Oldman was looking for help.

Fort Wagner could very well have been a powder keg looking to explode.

He followed Katherine Downing to a table set up for registration in the tournament.

"Gonna sign up, little lady?" the man behind the table asked.

"I am," Clint said.

"Ain't got no women yet," the man said. "Thought you might like to try."

"No," she said gently, "just him."

Clint noticed that Katherine was attracting a lot of attention now. She pulled her shawl tightly around her.

"Well, sign away, fella," the man said.

Clint signed his name and was given a tally sheet where his winnings would be officially recorded.

"Katherine?"

Clint straightened and looked to see who had called her name. He saw a tall, well-dressed man with a carefully trimmed mustache approaching with a smile on his handsome face.

"Victor," she said.

"My dear," the man said, grabbing both of her hands in his, "what are you doing here?"

"My friend is entering the tournament."

"Your friend?"

The man looked at Clint.

"Clint Adams," she said, "meet Victor Marks. Victor owns the Red Hand."

"Mr. Marks."

The man extended his hand and looked at Clint with interest.

"Of course I know who Mr. Adams is. You honor our little tournament."

"I wouldn't want you to, uh, announce that I'm here," Clint said.

"No, of course not, but we will be posting the names of all the entrants."

"That's fine."

"What brings you to Fort Wagner?" Marks asked, releasing his hand. "Certainly not this tournament."

"No, I didn't even know about it. I was just passing through."

"And it attracted your interest?"

"I asked Clint to play, Victor."

"You?" Marks gave her a puzzled look. Clint had the feeling that something was going on here that he didn't know about.

"I need the money."

"My dear," Marks said, "I've offered to buy—"

"I know, Victor."

"Or loan—"

"I prefer not to borrow money, Victor," she said, interrupting him again, "you know that."

Clint had the feeling that she just didn't want to borrow money from Victor Marks.

"Mr. Marks?" the man behind the table said.

"Yes?"

"We're ready, sir," he said. "Mr., uh, Adams was the last to register."

"All right, Leo," Marks said. "We'll get started." He turned to Clint and said, "I wish you luck."

"Thanks."

Marks walked off and Clint looked at Katherine.

"Something you forgot to tell me?"

"He wants to buy the hotel," she said. "I think he's glad I'm not doing well because he thinks I'll sell."

"He's not going to be too happy if I win this thing,"
Clint said.

"I guess not."

"What would he do?"

"What could he do?" she asked. "He has to pay
you."

"I meant, what would he do *after* he paid me?"

"Oh." She looked crestfallen. "Have I put you in
danger?"

"That's what I'd like to know," he said. Then he
softened the blow of his words by adding, "Don't
worry. Everything will work out."

A voice called out for all the players to come to the
tables.

She touched his arm and said, "Good luck."

"Thanks."

TWENTY-FIVE

On the second night of John Duggin's patrol of Brazzleton's streets and back alleys, the killer was starting to get frustrated at having to wait for his next kill. He and his men had been scouring the town for the last two nights with nothing to show for it.

The night before, after he called off his hunt, he had gone to the same whorehouse that Weller and Kylie were at. There he had picked out a buxom little brunette named Jodi Caller and had enjoyed her company immensely. She hadn't even minded when he hurt her a little. He was looking forward to seeing her again tonight.

When he quit his second night of searching, he went to the whorehouse again. He didn't notice how she cringed when she saw him enter.

Jodi came over to him in the parlor and rubbed up against him. He allowed her to take his hand and lead him up to her room and her satin-sheeted bed.

"Did my baby miss me?" she asked.

"Yeah, yeah." Duggin hated wasting time while on a job. He could smell his prey near, he just couldn't find them. He took off his jacket, exposing the double-rig shoulder holster. He went to the door to close it.

"That you, John?"

The familiar voice instantly caught his attention. He stepped out into the hall and faced the man who had called to him. It was Luke Kylie. He was standing in the doorway of a room almost directly across from Jodi's.

"I thought that was you when you went by. Any luck?"

"No," Duggin said. "How long have you been here?"

"About half an hour," Kylie said. "I didn't find nothing tonight, either."

"Where's Weller?"

"Still lookin', I guess."

Duggin lifted his shoulders to feel the weight of his twin .45's under his arms.

"Tomorrow we're gonna get those two. I'm tired of coming up empty with all three of us searching this stinkin' town from top to bottom."

Kylie, dressed only in long johns, looked over his shoulder at the naked blonde on the bed. She was combing her hair and staring off into space with a blank look on her face.

"John, what if they're not here?"

"They're here."

"What if they were here but they moved on—"

"They're here, Luke," Duggin said loudly. "I can smell 'em. They're here, and tomorrow we'll find them."

"Take it easy, John—"

"Don't tell me to take it easy!"

Before Kylie could reply, the door to the room next to his swung open. Popping his head out from his darkened room, Kylie's neighbor looked angrily out into the hall.

"Will you two shut the hell up and give a man some peace and quiet?"

The man's words halted the two assassins' conversation as both of them turned to see who had spoken. Although it took "Killer" Duggin a minute to see the man's features clearly in the dim hallway, he immediately recognized the angry man.

It took Luke Kylie a few seconds longer to realize that one of the men they were hunting for was right next door. He saw Duggin's face turn into a mask of pure joy as he reached for both of his guns.

The neighbor looked to be in his late twenties, with a smooth face and slender build. A rumpled mop of brown hair hung over his eyes.

"That's Andy Crawford!" Kylie shouted, but Duggin was way ahead of him.

By the time Duggin's pistols cleared leather, Andy Crawford realized what was happening and ducked back into the room. As he hit the floor, he covered his head with his hands, as if this would protect him from the coming attack.

Enthralled by the excitement of finding one of his prey, Duggin fired both pistols at the same time, sending half a dozen slugs into the door and door frame of Crawford's room. When he overcame his initial flurry of emotion, Duggin lowered the gun in his left hand, allowing himself to more carefully fire the one in his right.

Luke Kylie lunged over the bed—and the blonde on

it—in his room, reaching for the shotgun in the corner of the room.

"What's goin' on, Luke?" the girl asked, her voice filled with fear.

"Shut up!"

After making sure his weapon was loaded, he crept over to the wall that divided his room from Crawford's. Luke listened to Crawford scrambling on the floor when Duggin's initial flurry ended. Quickly he figured out where his target was in the other room, pressed the barrel of his gun against the thin, wooden wall, and fired.

The shot blasted a hole through the wall and made the woman in Kylie's bed cower down under the covers. Bits of wood and paint from the wall rained down on her, littering the bed.

Kylie looked through the hole and saw Andy Crawford huddled on the floor through a haze of gun smoke. Wanting to cover his boss from a better angle, he got to his feet and ran into the hall.

TWENTY-SIX

Andy Crawford couldn't move, even if his life depended on it . . . which it did. When he finally mustered the nerve to go for the gun hanging on the bedpost, the wall to his left exploded with a deafening roar. The blast froze him for the next few seconds, but self-preservation finally gave him the strength to go for the gun again. Before he could reach it, though, John Duggin stepped into the room and fired a bullet into his shoulder from behind. Crawford screamed and fell to the floor face first. The red-haired girl on his bed screamed and pulled her knees up to her ample chest.

Duggin smiled as he stepped further into the room and surveyed the situation. He was in complete control now.

"Finally we meet, Andy."

The Killer looked over at the bed and saw Crawford's companion cowering there. When she saw him watching her, she unwrapped her arms from around her knees so she could straighten her legs out, revealing large, rounded breasts.

"Ma'am," Duggin said, tipping his hat to the lady.

He holstered his gun and walked over to where Crawford was lying, moaning and cursing. He sent a boot into the fallen man's ribs, teeth clenched in a wicked smile.

Kylie was covering the action from the doorway, still standing in the hall with his shotgun ready. He had already reloaded.

"You're a hard man to find, Andy," Duggin said.

Another kick in the same spot broke one of Crawford's ribs. From the hall he suddenly heard a door slam open and another voice calling out.

"I'm comin', Andy. Hold on, buddy!"

Quickly, Kylie stepped into the room and flattened himself against the door.

Dwight Dixon was larger than his friend and looked to be about five or six years older. His face was covered with a scraggly beard and mustache, covering a nasty scar on his chin.

As Dixon came rushing through the doorway, Kylie lifted his shotgun and rammed the butt of it into the center of the man's face. Dixon's nose exploded and sent blood flying all over. He had a gun in his hand, which he dropped to the floor, and then he fell to his knees, his hands over his face, trying to staunch the flow of blood.

Duggin looked over at Dixon and nodded his satisfaction to Kylie.

"Guess we don't need this one," he said, and fired a bullet into the back of Andy Crawford's head.

He turned to Kylie and said, "Get him up."

Kylie reached down and yanked Dixon to his feet. The man got his legs under him as Kylie pushed him over to the window. He pressed the barrel of his shotgun against the man's back, forcing him up against the glass.

"Where's the rest of them?" Duggin asked.

The man said something which might have been, "I don't know," but it was altered by his smashed nose and the blood still flowing from it.

"If you don't answer, my friend is going to blow your spine out the window," Duggin said. "I'll ask again, and speak real slow so we can understand you. Where are the others?"

"I—I don't know . . . where Whiteoak is . . . but Sage Johnson is in—"

"Sage is dead," Duggin said. "Try again."

"Last I heard," Dixon said, "two of 'em were in Fort Wagner. It's in West Texas. Uh, Jimmy Meade and Mike Kimnach headed there for some kind of poker tournament. They should still be there."

Duggin doubted the man was lying. He was too frightened for that.

"And Whiteoak?"

"I told you, I don't know where—"

"Try again."

Kylie pushed the barrel of the shotgun deeper into the man's back.

"All I know is he got hisself a wagon . . ." the man blubbered.

"What kind of wagon?"

"I don't . . . wait, wait . . . it was all painted up, like a carnival wagon. That's it! With red letters."

"Red letters," Duggin said. "That shouldn't be too hard to find."

"Will you let me go now?" the man pleaded.

"Sure." Duggin nodded to Kylie, who was surprised and pleased at being allowed the kill. "Help him out the window, Luke."

Kylie pulled the trigger and the front of Dwight Dixon exploded, most of his insides flying out the window in a shower of red spray and glass, followed by his lifeless body.

Duggin turned to Kylie and said, "Find Weller. We're gettin' out tonight."

"What are you gonna do?"

Duggin looked at the whore on the bed and thought about the two in the other rooms and said, "Take care of some unfinished business."

Within an hour the three assassins were saddled up and riding out of Brazzleton. Along the way Duggin and Kylie filled Weller in on what they'd found out.

"Wish I'd been there to see him fly out that window," Weller said. "Must've been a sight."

Duggin didn't hear what he was saying. He was thinking about the three dead whores he'd left on one of the beds in one of the rooms. There'd be some commotion when they were found, but he couldn't very well leave them behind to identify him and Kylie, could he?

That just wouldn't have been good business.

TWENTY-SEVEN

On Clint's second day in Fort Wagner, he decided to take a walk around the town that had changed so much since he was last there. After cleaning up and having breakfast in the hotel dining room, he came out into the lobby and saw Katherine behind the desk. She had not been there when he first came down.

"Good morning," he said, approaching the desk.

She looked up from her work and brightened when she saw him.

"How did you do last night?" she asked. "I got tired and had to leave."

"Last night was just a get-acquainted session," he said. "The real playing starts tonight."

In point of fact he had made about fifty dollars last night, but the stakes had simply been one dollar to five. The tournament game was five-card stud, and normally the stakes in a five-card game were higher than that— at least, when he played in other games they were. This

109

was to account for less playing rounds than a seven-card game or a draw poker game.

"But are you ahead?"

"Far enough ahead to pay for dinner tonight."

"Oh, no," she said, "that's part of our bargain."

"All right, then," he said. "The game starts at eight. Dinner at six?"

"I'll be here," she said. "What are you going to do today?"

"Just get reacquainted with the town."

"Well, be careful," she said. "I don't want anything happening to you. I have a big investment in your health."

"I'll try to keep that in mind."

He spent the better part of the morning walking around town, and as the sun climbed inexorably to its zenith he saw Sheriff Oldman coming toward him.

"I saw you last night," Oldman said, "in the Red Hand. I thought you weren't interested in the poker game."

"So did I," Clint said. "Let me buy you a beer and I'll tell you what happened."

"I could use one about now," Oldman said.

They went into a nearby saloon that was considerably smaller than the Red Hand. It was called the Texan.

After Clint told him how he got roped into the tournament, the sheriff sympathized—but also tried to use the situation to his own advantage.

"I can't blame you," he said, "I'd let Katherine Downing talk me into anything . . . but do me a favor, will you?"

"That depends on what it is."

"Since you're gonna be in the tournament anyway, keep your eyes on things, will you?"

"I told you, Sheriff, I'm not interested in being a deputy—"

"I'm not askin' you to be a deputy," Oldman said. "Just watch for trouble around you. Play your game and do your business, but let people know who you are. Folks will be less likely to start trouble if they know the Gunsmith is around."

"First off, I don't like that name," Clint said.

"But I thought—"

"Second, I don't particularly want to announce to the general public who I am."

"I only meant—"

"I know what you meant," Clint said. "Now I'll tell you what I will do. If trouble arises anywhere near me, I'll do what I can to stop it. That's all I can offer."

"I'll accept that offer," Oldman said. "Thank you for it, and for the beer."

With a shrug and a halfhearted wave, Sheriff Oldman turned and left the saloon. Clint could sympathize with the man's plight, but letting people know who he was usually brought gunmen out of the walls, instead of keeping them away. He'd do what he said, though. He'd be on the lookout for trouble. He didn't want anything interfering with him winning this tournament for Katherine Downing. He was counting on her being *very* grateful to him.

Sheriff Oldman had heard all of the legends about Clint Adams. When he had originally requested some help from the county seat for this poker tournament crowd, he'd hoped for someone with one half—hell, one *tenth* of Clint Adams's experience. When he realized who Adams was last night, he thought his prayers had been answered.

Instead, Clint had refused to be a deputy. Thank God for Katherine Downing and her charms. At least the Gunsmith would be around, and Oldman knew that if there was any trouble, the man would back him.

That was part of his reputation.

TWENTY-EIGHT

For the past few days Henry Whiteoak had been trying to follow Clint Adams's trail from Wider's Canyon. He thought it would be easy enough to acquaint himself with the surrounding area and figure out where the man was going. He'd used this method before in finding people.

This time, however, it was a different story. Trailing Clint Adams required a lot more caution than trailing anyone else. Whiteoak knew that the man would not appreciate it. Because of this he hadn't wanted to get too close, and because of *that* he had to admit that he'd lost the man's trail.

For a man with the professor's pride and self-worth, admitting this—even to himself—was not an easy thing to do. When he finally gave up, he decided that he might as well meet up with some friends of his. After all, his attempt to find Clint Adams had brought him well within range of Fort Wagner.

Last he'd heard, some old partners of his were there,

probably hoping to win some money in the town's poker tournament. What used to be an annual event had turned into a monthly thing, or pretty near. He, himself, had played in it and won a couple of times, so he knew when it was scheduled for. He wondered how Victor Marks would react to seeing him in the tournament again. Then again, he might have missed it by a day or two. He'd find out for sure when he got there.

Whiteoak had always been a gambler. It was in his blood. So was being a con man. There was nothing he could do about it but put it to his advantage.

Urging his wagon and team toward Fort Wagner, the medicine man shifted in his seat and settled in for a half a day's ride. Letting his mind wander, he thought about the ex-partners he'd be meeting there.

James Meade was as slick a liar as there ever was. He could fast-talk his way in or out of any situation. Mike Kimnach was as accomplished an actor as Whiteoak had ever approached. Originally a stage actor, he found the confines of the stage too binding. Off the stage he could step into any role, such as the mayor of a town with the rights to many ranch deeds.

He wondered if Joe Halsey was still looking for all of them. Maybe it was time to put the team back together for another big score. He was getting tired of the medicine man act.

Hell, he thought, with Meade and Kimnach he wouldn't even need a Clint Adams.

Although having a man like that on his side certainly wouldn't hurt.

While Clint was checking on Duke in the livery stable, he felt as if he'd stepped out of the constant motion that made up life in Fort Wagner and stepped into the only calm place in town.

"Well, I did it again, old boy," he said, patting the gelding's neck. "I'm coming to the rescue of another damsel in distress. How do I get myself involved in these things, huh?"

Duke just shook his head, and Clint took this to mean that the big black gelding didn't know the reason any more than he did.

He left the livery and headed back to the Texas Grand. Katherine Downing was behind the desk, and he walked to it and leaned on it.

"You're early," she said, smiling.

"I'm impatient," he said. "I could go upstairs and clean up and be back down here in twenty minutes. We could have an early dinner."

"Hmm," Katherine said, "give me forty minutes and you have a deal."

As Katherine watched Clint climb the stairs, she smiled to herself. She was thinking she might end up getting more involved with Clint Adams than she had originally thought. She was taken from her reverie by the appearance of a potential guest.

She knew by his look that he was a gambler. In fact, she thought she might have recognized him from another time, another tournament. He wore a long black coat over his suit, which almost concealed a pistol strapped to his side.

"Well, good day, ma'am," Henry Whiteoak said pleasantly. "What are my chances of getting a room this afternoon?"

TWENTY-NINE

As the night wore on Clint realized that he had never heard of the Fort Wagner poker tournament. Katherine had told him at dinner that it had become a monthly function, due to the efforts of Victor Marks.

He did not see a single top-notch gambler at any of the tables, and the stakes were certainly not what would attract a Bat Masterson or a Luke Short. Neither would any of them have trouble with the quality of players— at least, not the players at his table.

To put it bluntly, Clint was cleaning them out. None of them knew the subtle nuances of the game, and none of them seemed to know the subtle nuances of a *bath*. One by one they fell by the wayside, losing their original buy-in and having to step aside. Before long, Clint was the last player at the table. He looked at the other tables and saw that they were still competitive.

"Looks like you get a break, mister," his dealer said.

"Looks like."

"Why don't you get yourself a drink. We'll come and get you when another place opens up."

"Fine."

Clint got up to walk to the bar and stopped short when he heard a familiar voice. It was a distinct, booming voice from the recent past and he was not happy to hear it. Searching for the source, he finally found where the man was, standing at the bar, holding forth in a group of men, telling one tall tale or another, or maybe trying to sell them something.

Henry Whiteoak.

Clint walked to the bar, and from the look on White-oak's face he was just as surprised to see Clint as Clint was to see him. Was he acting? Had he, indeed, followed Clint here to try to follow up on their discussion about a partnership? Clint thought he had closed the door on that possibility very firmly.

"Whiteoak, what the hell are you doing here?"

"Well, that's a fine greeting for a friend."

"Whiteoak—"

"I came for the tournament, just as you did," White-oak said, "but apparently I'm a day late. So, I am reduced to being a spectator."

Somehow, Clint did not see Whiteoak in the role of spectator.

"You didn't follow me here, did you?"

Since Whiteoak had lost Clint's trail, he could honestly say, "Why, no, I did not. I assure you."

"Well, then, spectate all you want, but stay away from me, understand?"

"Perfectly . . . of course, if you would let me buy you a drink to make up for, ah, past grievances—"

"Just stay away from me," Clint said coldly.

"Fine," Whiteoak said, "if you wish to rebuff my friendship, that is your . . ."

Clint walked away from whatever else Whiteoak had to say and found himself another spot at the bar.

Clint kept his eye on Whiteoak and saw two men approach him during a break in the action of the tournament. They greeted each other as friends would, which surprised him. Anyone who knew Whiteoak well enough to consider becoming friends would know him well enough *not* to. These two men, however, seemed very glad to see him.

James Meade was the same age as Whiteoak, but his hair had turned prematurely gray. He had the soft, round body of a man who had lived the easy life, but Whiteoak knew him to be the possessor of a most silvery tongue, so he rarely had the need to defend himself physically when he could talk himself out of any situation.

Mike Kimnach was younger than both Whiteoak and Meade, but actually looked older than he was. That was how he'd been able to play the part of a town mayor in the Joe Halsey con—that and some actor's makeup.

Kimnach stood a few inches shorter than the other two con men, but his smaller body was brawnier than either of theirs.

"Saw you come in, Henry," Meade said, shaking hands. "You're a day late for this."

"So I understand. How are you boys doing?"

"Holding our own," Kimnach said. "What brings you here, Henry, really? You're not here for the game."

"That gentleman over there is what brought me here, boys," Whiteoak said.

"Which one?" Meade asked, turning to look.

"The one scowling at me, holding a beer mug."

"He's in the tournament," Meade said. "Cleaned out his table."

"It's no wonder," Whiteoak said. "That, gents, is Clint Adams."

"Holy shit!" Kimnach said, lowering his voice. "The Gunsmith? Is he after you, Henry? Christ, if he's after you, you're as good as—"

"No, no, nothing like that," Whiteoak said. "Actually, he helped me out of some trouble a short time back and I offered him a partnership."

"And?" Meade asked.

"He refused."

"Why?"

Whiteoak shrugged.

"It seems he doesn't like me."

"Ah," Meade said, "someone who didn't fall for your charm, eh?"

"Something like that."

"Jesus," Kimnach said, "but that's the Gunsmith—"

"Lower your voice," Meade hissed at him.

"But what if Halsey sent him—" Kimnach said. The youngest of the three, he was the one who was still looking over his shoulder.

"He wouldn't work for the likes of Joe Halsey," Whiteoak said.

"How can you be sure?" Kimnach asked.

"I know the man, Mike," Whiteoak said. "Take my word for it. Besides, Halsey's probably forgotten all about us."

He and Meade exchanged a glance that said both men knew that wasn't true, but he was trying to allay the younger man's fears.

"Let me tell you fellas about my first meeting with Clint Adams," Whiteoak said.

"Make it quick," Meade said. "The game's gonna start up again soon."

"It don't matter," Kimnach said. "I'm about out of it anyway."

"I'll make it quick . . ." Whiteoak said, but he'd never told a story without embellishments in his life. Colorfully, he related the incidents leading up to his meeting with Clint.

"That's quite a story," Meade said, knowing that he should take anything Whiteoak said with a little grain of salt. Suffice it to say he believed that Whiteoak and Clint Adams had met.

"Just think," Whiteoak said, "what we could do with him by our side."

"If he wouldn't work for the likes of Joe Halsey," Meade said, "what makes you think he'd work with the likes of you?"

"Why would we need him?" Kimnach asked.

"Because," Whiteoak said slowly, "people respect him, they listen to him, and—most importantly—they would *believe* him."

James Meade shook his head as the call went out for the players to return to their tables.

"He'll never do it."

"We'll see," Whiteoak said, "we'll see."

As the two men left Whiteoak to go back to their table, they were staring at Clint. He knew this meant that he'd been the subject of their conversation, at least in part. What had Whiteoak told them?

"Mr. Adams?"

Clint looked at the man and recognized him as one of the dealers.

"We have a place for you now."

"Fine," Clint said, "fine."

He tried to put Whiteoak out of his mind and followed the dealer to one of the tables.

THIRTY

By the time John Duggin reined his horse to a stop on the outskirts of Fort Wagner, he and his men were ready to find a hole and crawl into it. The three had been riding for the last few days without one meal or a good night's sleep between them, except for their one night in Caterville—and none of them had gotten very much sleep spending that night in a whorehouse.

Duggin knew his men were tired, but he'd been pushing them anyway. The money at the end of this job would be enough for all of them to kick back for a good long time. Besides, Duggin never believed in putting off killing somebody.

As the Killer sat in his saddle and stared at the town in front of them, Jeremiah Weller sidled up next to him.

"Are we goin' into town?"

"You know what your problem is, Weller?"

"Uh . . . no."

"I'll tell you. You don't know how to savor the little moments in life."

Luke Kylie, still riding behind the other two, rolled his eyes and rubbed his temples with dusty hands. He knew the speech that was coming because he used to hear it a lot when he first started riding with Duggin.

"Times like these are the best you'll ever find. It's like chasing a woman. You know she's out there. The question is whether or not you'll get her to roll over for you."

Kylie tried to tune Duggin out, but he was unsuccessful.

"Looking forward to the action is almost as good as the action itself. It's that way with women . . . and it's that way with killin'."

Kylie knew John Duggin well enough to know that he'd rather wrap his hands around his twin .45's than around the breasts of a woman.

He also liked to talk.

"All right," Duggin said, spurring his horse on, "let's get goin'."

From behind his desk Joe Halsey planned the expansion of his land holdings. In front of him were the deeds to three properties. Ever since he'd been made a fool of by Henry Whiteoak, Halsey vowed to never be tricked again.

Instead of trusting any of his land scouts, Halsey now visited each piece of property personally. If he'd gained anything from his encounter with Whiteoak, he'd learned to be more careful.

He'd also learned to hate a person more than he thought he ever could. More than anything Halsey wanted to look at Whiteoak's face one more time, put a gun to his head, and pull the trigger. In his life he'd only ever killed one man, and at that time there had been no thrill. In fact, he had felt sick after it.

This time he knew that killing Henry Whiteoak was going to be the thrill of his life.

At the end of three days Clint was ahead two thousand dollars. As the number of tables decreased, the amount of the bets increased.

He left the saloon this night with his senses alert. The more money he made, the more vigilant he had to be. He was sure there were men in town who had come simply to get rich off poker winnings—by stealing them from other people. He had no intention of letting that happen to him.

Suddenly he heard footsteps approaching behind him and a metallic sound. In a quick, fluid motion that had once been practiced and was now second nature to him he turned and drew his gun.

"Oh, my God!"

He was looking into the horrified face of Katherine Downing.

THIRTY-ONE

Clint put the Colt back in his holster and stared at her.

"Don't ever sneak up on me like that."

"I'll make a note of it," she said, pressing one hand to her chest. She was trying to get her breath back from the scare.

"What do you have in your other hand, Katherine?" he asked.

She showed him a key ring with some keys on it, which had been banging together, causing the metallic sound he'd heard.

"What are those?"

"Keys, silly."

"I can see that," he said. "Keys to what?"

"To the livery stable."

"Why do you have keys to the livery stable?"

"Because there are times when my guests need to get to their horses late at night," she said. "Benny—he's the owner—gave me a set of keys."

"Well, why are you on your way to the livery stable now?"

"Because," she said, taking his hand, "it's empty."

"Wha—"

"Come on, Clint," she said. "Don't play hard to get. Come on!"

He allowed her to pull him along until they reached the livery. She released his hand and unlocked the door, which he swung open. They stepped inside and he closed the door behind them.

A shaft of moonlight came in from a small window in the ceiling. Walking through that beam of light Katherine almost seemed to glow.

Clint could see that this was very calculated on her part. She turned to face him and, standing directly in that shaft of light, began to undress. His mouth went dry and he was unable to look away.

Katherine's flowing black hair cascaded over her shoulders, covering all but the full, rounded bottoms of her breasts. Her hips were full curves that traced a line down to smooth, muscular legs. Taking in the sight of her, Clint found himself unable to speak. Also, he could wait for her no longer.

As though she could feel his growing tension, Katherine strode to him and began to peel him out of his clothes. When she was done she cupped him in her hands, stroking his cock as she gazed hungrily into his eyes.

"How badly do you want me?" she asked.

He smiled and said, "About as badly as you want me."

She laughed and said, "Good answer," and pulled him toward a pile of blankets in one of the empty stalls.

He turned her around so he could cup her luscious

breasts from behind, hefting their weight in his palms, thumbing the nipples. She sighed and allowed her head to fall to one side so he could kiss her neck and shoulders.

She turned then and bore him down to the blankets, lying him on his back. She straddled him immediately, but did not allow him to enter her. Instead she rubbed herself against him, trapping his rigid cock between them, wetting it. While she ground herself against him, she leaned over him, surrounding his face with the sweet scent of her hair.

As she continued to tease him with her slow grind, Clint alternated between taking her nipples in his mouth and running his tongue between her swinging breasts. Before he could do anything else, she crawled up on him so that the soft patch of hair between her legs was directly over his mouth.

Clint gently kissed the tender flesh of her thighs before lifting his head to enter her with his tongue.

"Oh, my God, Clint . . . my God . . ." Katherine moaned as she rocked on his face.

As he worked on her with his mouth, she began biting the back of her hand to keep from crying out.

She stayed in that position until she couldn't bear it anymore, until they both could no longer put off what they yearned for.

Katherine moved down his body until she was crotch to crotch with him, and then reached between them to guide him inside her, impaling herself on him.

For a few strokes she slowly rocked on him, letting her hair brush his chest and neck, savoring every inch of his hardness as it eased in and out of her, again and again. As she began to speed up, Clint reached around and grabbed hold of her firm ass, pulling her even more tightly against him.

Suddenly she reached down and dug her nails into his chest, her body tensing with the oncoming rush of ecstasy. He felt it, too, and the feeling of her closing around him like a wet, warm glove brought him to the brink that much sooner.

When her pleasure built almost to its climax, she locked her mouth over his and kissed him with all the passion she could muster. It was as if she were trying to breathe her passion into him—of which there was no need. He had enough of his own.

When she reached her peak, she moaned loudly into his mouth. If they hadn't been kissing he thought she might have screamed.

Later, as their passion subsided, Katherine held her face over Clint's, allowing her flowing hair to surround them.

"Good Lord," he said when he caught his breath.

"The feeling is mutual, sweetie," she said, kissing him.

Katherine climbed off him and lay down beside him.

"We can't stay here," she said.

"I don't think I can move yet."

"Well, you better move, mister."

She stood up, picked up his clothes, and tossed them to him.

"Why?" he asked.

"Because," she said, starting to dress, "I've always wanted to try that big bed in the Presidential Suite."

THIRTY-TWO

When Clint woke the next morning Katherine was sound asleep next to him. Even with both of them in the bed it was so big he had room to ease away from her without waking her, then roll over to the other side to get up. It was easily the largest bed Clint had ever been in, and they had made full use of every inch of it.

"At least now the damned thing is worth what I paid to have it hauled from back east," she had said at one point.

When he was halfway dressed she stirred and looked up at him.

"Mmmm, Clint . . . what time is it?"

He looked out the window and said, "I think it's about nine. I don't usually sleep this late."

Oh," she said, rubbing her face with one hand, "I have to get to work."

"You're the boss," he said.

"And the only full-time employee."

She got out of bed and he watched with pleasure as

she searched for her dress and eventually found it under the bed.

"God," she said, "I can't wear this again." She looked at him and asked, "Could you do me a favor?"

"What is it?"

"Could you go down, unlock the front door, and man the desk while I get myself around? I won't be long."

"I've never worked in a hotel."

"There's nothing to it. If a guest comes in, just let them sign the register and give them a key. I promise, I won't be long."

Somehow he didn't think that her definition of "long" was the same as his, but he agreed.

He left the room and started downstairs, thinking that life was full of new experiences.

Although it had been at least a half an hour and Katherine had not yet appeared, Clint found that he didn't mind. He was reading yesterday's newspaper and no one had come in looking for a room. Now he knew why so many desk clerks fell asleep on the job.

As Clint turned the pages of the newspaper, the front door opened and a scruffy-looking man entered. He could have just come in from the trail, but somehow Clint doubted it. While he was grimy, there was no fresh trail dust on him. Clint just thought that the man was badly in need of a bath and a change of clothes.

"Can I help you?" he asked.

Without a word the man came to the desk, turned the register around, and began to scan it. Apparently, he found what he wanted because his face lit up like a kid's on Christmas morning.

"Excuse me," Clint said. "Do you want a room?"

"Yeah," the man said, "I want room 212."

Clint turned and looked at the board and saw that room 212 was occupied. When he turned back, the man had produced a shotgun from beneath his long coat. Clint realized then and there that he had made the biggest mistake of his life—and possibly his last.

He had left his gun upstairs.

He figured he must really be getting old—and possibly no older than the next few moments.

"Don't try anything cute and I won't blow your guts all over the wall."

"Sounds like a good deal."

"Smart man," Luke Kylie said.

"What do you want?"

"I want your key to room 212. You're gonna take me up there."

Clint looked down at the register and saw that room 212 was occupied by none other than Henry Whiteoak.

What was this supernatural connection between him, Whiteoak, and trouble?

"Make up your mind," the man said.

Clint grabbed the extra key for 212 and said, "Right this way."

THIRTY-THREE

Heading toward the stairs with Luke Kylie right behind him, Clint wasn't surprised that someone like this would want to kill Henry Whiteoak. He also knew that, no matter how he felt about the man, he couldn't just let it happen.

"What do you want with Henry Whiteoak?" he asked as they started up the stairs.

"He's a good friend of mine," Kylie said, "and I want to surprise him."

Clint thought that the shotgun-wielding man would be more than a little surprise for the professor.

Without another word Clint led the way to the second floor. He walked straight to Whiteoak's room, still trying to figure out what he could do in the face of a shotgun with no gun of his own.

Fitting the key into the lock he was going to jiggle it as a warning until the man with the shotgun said in a low voice, "If you make any noise I'll blow your spine out your chest."

132

That would open the door, Clint found himself thinking.

Clint inched the door open and peered inside. To his relief the room was empty. Whiteoak had probably risen early and gone out for breakfast.

"He's not home," Clint said.

"Inside," Luke Kylie said, and pushed Clint into the room. Standing just inside the doorway the man looked around for himself.

"See?"

"Yeah, I see," Kylie said. "Did the fella who rented this room show up with any friends?"

Clint thought about the two men he'd seen in the saloon with Whiteoak, but they hadn't arrived with him.

"Not that I know of."

"Whataya mean, not that you know of? You work here, don't you?"

"As a matter of fact, I don't," Clint said.

"Then what were you doing behind the desk?"

"I was just helping out a friend."

"Yeah, well," Luke Kylie said, "that's your tough luck, ain't it?"

Kylie raised his shotgun to fire it, and Clint tensed to make what he was sure would be a futile leap.

"Excuse me, gents, but what are you doing in my—?" The voice came from behind the gunman, and stopped short when the speaker realized something was wrong.

Clint's chances for survival had suddenly improved as the voice attracted Kylie's attention for just a split second.

Lunging for Kylie's shotgun, Clint dove across the space between them and grabbed the barrel of the weapon, just as it went off in his hands. Clint felt the burn of the gun's blast as it started a high-pitched ringing in his ears.

Henry Whiteoak still stood in the hallway, staring at Luke Kylie with wide, disbelieving eyes. The sound of the shot snapped him out of his stunned silence and he dove for Kylie's legs.

The impact of Whiteoak's tackle caused Kylie to loosen his grip on the shotgun, and Clint wrenched it from his hands before he could fire it again. Whiteoak got to his feet and launched a punch that landed squarely on Kylie's jaw. The punch snapped the man's head back, sending him staggering into the room, where he fell over Clint, who was on his knees. As Kylie went over him Clint reared up, adding impetus to the man's progress. Kylie went flying into a wall. He slammed against it and lay there, stunned.

"You all right, Adams?" Whiteoak asked.

Clint wasn't all right. His right hand had been badly burned, but he didn't want to tell anyone that.

"I'm fine," he said, holding the shotgun in his left hand. "This fella was looking for you. Do you know him?"

Whiteoak looked down at Luke Kylie, who he certainly did know, and said, "No, never saw him before."

Kylie stirred and tried to regain his senses. He looked up and saw the two men standing across from him. They were between him and the door, so he saw only one way out of the situation.

"Look out!" Whiteoak shouted as Kylie sprang from his position.

Clint turned and made ready to receive the man's charge, but Kylie had fooled them both. Instead of going for the door he went for the window and launched himself through it. Broken glass flew out the window ahead of him as he landed on the low roof out there, then rolled and fell off, hitting the ground below.

Clint rushed to the window and saw the man running across the street, dragging his right leg.

"He got away," Whiteoak said, secretly pleased. He didn't want Kylie telling Clint about Joe Halsey.

"Who the hell was that?"

"I don't know."

Clint turned to look at Whiteoak.

"He was after you," he said. "Why?"

"Could be a lot of reasons. A lot of people don't like me."

"Don't I know it!"

Whiteoak looked hurt.

"Is that any way to talk to the man who saved your life?"

Clint paused as he realized Whiteoak was right.

"Yes, you did save my life, and I thank you for it," he said. "But I think you know more than you're telling, Whiteoak."

"I guess it's a good thing I went looking for a bath when I did," the medicine man said. "And also a good thing I didn't find one. Uh, nobody was working downstairs. Are you acquainted with the management?"

Clint knew the man was changing the subject, but he needn't have tried to. Katherine Downing came running into the room then, and when she saw the damaged window she put her hands on her hips and glared at the two men.

"What's been going on here?" she demanded. "Who broke my window?"

Quickly, Clint explained to Katherine what had happened.

"And he knows who the man was?" she asked, indicating Whiteoak.

"He says he doesn't," Clint said, "but I say he does."

"Then he's lying?"

"Dear lady—"

"Lying is something he does as easily as breathing."

"My good friend—"

"Shut up, Whiteoak," Clint said. "I'm willing to bet that man didn't come after you alone. If I'm right, then you need my help."

"You would help me?" Whiteoak asked.

Clint gritted his teeth and said, "In spite of my better judgment, yes—but you have to tell me the truth."

Whiteoak thought it over and then said, "Very well . . . but may I have another room? This one is bound to be a little . . . drafty?"

Clint looked at Katherine and said, "Why don't you give the man another room? That will give him and me someplace to talk."

"All right," she said. "Come downstairs and get a key—but you have to tell me what's going on, Clint."

"I will," Clint said, "just as soon as I find out."

Down in the lobby Katherine gave Whiteoak another key and asked Clint, "Do you think that man will come back?"

"I don't think so," Clint said, "not yet, anyway. Jumping out the window he hurt his leg. If he has partners he'll try to find them, and have them take care of his leg."

"Should I get the sheriff?"

"Not yet," Clint said. "Let me talk to Whiteoak first."

"Do you know Mr. Whiteoak?"

"We've had some dealings in the past, yes."

"Is he a friend?"

"No," Clint said, "he is most definitely not a friend."

Clint turned to Whiteoak, who had not heard what they were saying.

"Let's go, Whiteoak," Clint said, brandishing the new key. "You've got some explaining to do."

THIRTY-FOUR

Grudgingly, Henry Whiteoak told Clint about the entire chain of events that had brought Luke Kylie to the Texas Grand Hotel looking for him. Starting with the organization of his little group of con men, all the way to their flight from Halsey's men.

Clint ran his hands through his hair, frustrated at once again being involved with violence started by Henry Whiteoak.

"So that man with the shotgun works for Joe Halsey?" he asked.

"Actually, he works for John Duggin."

" 'Killer' Duggin?"

"That's what they call him," Whiteoak said. "John works for Halsey and now, apparently, they've found us."

"Us?"

"I don't mean you," Whiteoak said.

"Those two men I saw you with at the saloon? They were in on the con?"

138

Whiteoak nodded.

"Well, they have to be warned."

"I'll warn them."

"And then this is how it's going to be, Professor. You and your men are going to pack your things and get out of town before these assassins start shooting up the place."

"But why?"

"Why? So you don't get killed."

"But . . . you said you'd help me."

"I am," Clint said. "I'm giving you good advice."

"B-but I thought . . . you meant . . ."

"Meant what?"

"That you'd take care of John Duggin and his men for me."

Clint laughed out loud.

"You think I'm going to go up against Duggin and his men for you?"

"Well, you might not have a choice."

"What are you talking about?"

"Duggin's not gonna like what you did to his man," Whiteoak said. "By the way, his name is Luke Kylie."

"I never heard of him. Who else will be around?"

"Fella named . . . what is it . . . Weller, Jeremiah Weller."

"I don't know him, either."

Clint had heard of John "The Killer" Duggin, though. If only half of what he had heard was true, Duggin was a walking nightmare. But why should he put his life on the line against a man like Duggin for Henry Whiteoak? By conning a man like Joe Halsey, Whiteoak and his friends had brought this on themselves.

"Then you won't help me?" Whiteoak asked.

"Get yourself out of town, Whiteoak."

"And keep running, right? Keep looking over my shoulder?"

"You asked for it when you decided to bilk Joe Halsey out of his money."

"Jesus," Whiteoak said, looking distressed for the first time, "who thought he'd take it so hard? Nobody else ever did."

"Maybe you picked the wrong man this time."

"Clint, you've got to help me . . . Meade and Kimnach and me, we're no match for Duggin and his men."

Clint walked to the door.

"I've done what I can, Whiteoak."

"But I saved your life!"

"That makes us even," Clint said, "because if I remember correctly, I saved yours a while back, too."

With that Clint left the room, cutting Whiteoak's protestations off by closing the door.

"We've gotta get out of here now!"

Henry Whiteoak stormed into the hotel room James Meade and Mike Kimnach shared a few blocks away from the Texas Grand. After bursting through the door, Whiteoak went right to the window to check the street outside.

"What the hell are you talkin' about?" Kimnach demanded.

"They're here," Whiteoak said.

"Who?" Meade asked.

"John Duggin and his men."

"What?" Kimnach said.

"You saw Duggin?" Meade asked.

"I saw Luke Kylie. He came to my hotel with a shotgun, looking for me. If Kylie's here, Duggin is, too, or he ain't far behind."

"Jesus . . ." Meade said.

"We've got to warn the others—"

"Henry, I've got something to tell you," Meade said. "They're dead."

"What?"

"I heard from one of my contacts in Brazzleton. Crawford and Dixon were killed. I checked on Sage, and he's dead, too."

"My God . . . the man's a menace!" Whiteoak said.

"Duggin or Halsey?" Meade asked.

"Both!" Whiteoak said. "What kind of man has other men killed for money?"

"This has never happened to you before?" Meade asked. "With all the cons you've pulled?"

"No one has ever tried to kill me," Whiteoak said. "It's . . . it's just not natural."

Whiteoak was stunned by Meade's news as much as the other two men were stunned by his.

"Well, Henry," Meade said, "what do we do?"

Whiteoak looked at both men and said, "There's only one thing to do . . . run."

"If I know Whiteoak," John Duggin said as he led his men to the livery stable, "he'll be clearing out of town as fast as he can. We've got to act now, or lose him to another damn town."

"Duggin, Luke needs a doctor—"

"I'll tell you boys something," Duggin said, stopping short and turning on them. "If we lose these three while they're here together I'll kill both of you, instead."

Duggin had learned that Meade and Kimnach were in town, competing in the tournament. When Kylie came running up to him a little while ago with the news about Whiteoak, he decided that this would be the last stop on their hunt. After today, Joe Halsey would owe them a lot of money.

Knowing there was not an ounce of bluff in Duggin's words, Weller and Kylie simply nodded. Kylie decided that a sprained ankle was the least of his worries. He knew, however, that if he ever took his boot off his swollen foot he'd never get it back on.

The plan was simple: Duggin was to wait by White-oak's wagon, Weller would head back to the Texas Grand, and Kylie would go to the hotel where Meade and Kimnach were staying. Whenever the con men made a move to leave town they'd run into one of the killers.

"Now split up," Duggin said, "and remember, Whiteoak is worth more alive than dead."

When he reached the livery stable Duggin quickly sighted the brightly painted wagon. Spotting a shadowy corner from where he could watch, he knew he wouldn't have to wait long before his trap was sprung.

THIRTY-FIVE

With a large carpetbag in his hand, James Meade walked as quickly as he could out of his hotel. Mike Kimnach was inside, settling up their bill.

Kimnach came hurrying out behind him, grabbing his arm.

"Settle down, Jim," he said. "You want people to see us runnin'?"

"I don't care who sees us runnin', Mike, if it gets us away from Duggin and his men."

"Hey," Kimnach said, "we've got guns, too, you know."

"You want to stay behind and face Duggin, be my guest. I ain't afraid to say I ain't that brave—or stupid."

"Naw, I don't want to face him, either," Mike Kimnach said, "but if people see us runnin' down the street they're gonna remember us. We gotta walk, Jim. Take it easy, don't panic."

There was a shot right at that moment, and Mike Kimnach watched as James Meade's right eye disappeared, along with part of his head.

And he panicked.

Clint was in the lobby of the hotel with Katherine. She hadn't wanted to be alone there after what she heard about Duggin and his men.

"What if they come back?" she had asked.

"I don't think they will," Clint had said. "I think all the action is going to take place on the outside, now that everyone is aware of everyone else's presence."

"But what if they do?" she'd asked, so Clint decided to stay with her, even though what he really wanted to do was go and warn the sheriff.

They were together when they heard the shot. In that moment, Clint knew he couldn't just stand by and let Whiteoak and the others be gunned down by Duggin and his men. He started for the door.

"What are you doing?" Katherine asked.

"I have to take a look, Katherine," he said. "You'll be all right. Just stay inside."

Snapping out of the shock he experienced from seeing his friend killed in front of him, Mike Kimnach threw himself backward, into the hotel lobby. He dropped his bag and drew his gun. Outside he heard people shouting and running, trying to get off the street and out of harm's way.

In the lobby Kimnach crouched with his gun in his hands, his knees weak with fear. Was it Duggin himself out there, or one of his men?

As if to answer the question a man called out, "All right, Kimnach! Come on out before I have to come in after ya!"

At the same time as Clint Adams was leaving the hotel lobby, Henry Whiteoak was throwing his possessions into a large, leather case. Although he had no idea who had fired the shot he heard, he was willing to bet that Duggin and his men had something to do with it. If they were busy with Kimnach and Meade, maybe he could get away.

Finished with his packing, Whiteoak threw open the door to his new room and charged out into the hall. He hurried down the stairs leading to the lobby.

Sheriff Harve Oldman charged out of his office at the sound of the first shot. The tournament had been going on for three days, and he was surprised that someone hadn't been shot already. He knew that the quiet had been too good to be true.

As he ran down the street he passed the Texas Grand and saw Clint Adams come charging out.

"Do you know anything about this?" Oldman demanded.

"I might."

"Fill me in on the way," Oldman said. "You, uh, were coming out to help, weren't you?"

"Let's go," Clint said.

Luke Kylie stared down at the body of James Meade, the smoking Colt Peacemaker in his hand. The handgun had done the trick, though he missed his shotgun. After checking Meade, he had stopped and called his ultimatum to Mike Kimnach. The man had ignored him, and now he knew he'd have to go in after him. He couldn't afford to give the man time to get the bright idea of going out the back door. He still remembered Killer Duggin's promise.

Kylie eased his way toward the front of the hotel, limping on his bad ankle. After taking a deep breath, he entered the hotel where he knew Kimnach would not be looking . . . through the window next to the front door.

It was his day for going through windows.

THIRTY-SIX

Mike Kimnach crouched low under the large window in the hotel lobby, waiting for the assassin outside to make his move. With his gun trained on the door, he was ready for the unknown attacker to show himself.

Suddenly, the window above him shattered and Luke Kylie went sailing over his head. Glass rained down on him as he covered his head with his hands.

Kylie had it all planned. He was going to jump through the window, pivot, and fire. Even with just the handgun he'd be unlikely to miss at that range. Unfortunately, he made a crucial mistake. He kept his finger on the trigger when he jumped, and the landing jarred him so that he yanked on it. The Peacemaker went off, sending a bullet through the desk clerk, who had been too much in shock to duck the counter at the first sound of shooting.

Realizing what had happened, Kylie cursed and cocked his pistol again.

Kimnach took his hands from over his head, heard the

sound of the handgun being cocked, and grabbed for his gun.

Both men fired at the same time. Kylie's shot tore through Kimnach's shoulder, and Kimnach's shot just barely missed Kylie's head.

Kylie flinched as he heard Kimnach's shot whiz past his ear. Instead of firing again both men went for cover.

Kimnach ran to the desk and ducked behind it. He slipped on the blood on the floor and realized that the clerk had been killed by Kylie's initial shot. He was now stuck behind the desk with the dead body.

Kylie rolled behind the lobby sofa and reloaded his gun.

Both men were silent for just a moment, and in that silence they heard someone approach the hotel outside. From his vantage point Kimnach could see the sheriff looking down at James Meade's body.

"Sheriff, watch out!" he shouted.

"What the hell is going on?" Sheriff Oldman shouted.

He started for the door.

Clint had approached the hotel behind the sheriff, preferring to cover him that way. As they neared the hotel they had both seen the man on the ground.

"Jesus," Oldman had said, "who's that?"

"Be careful, Sheriff," Clint said, but the man did not seem to heed his warning. He marched up onto the boardwalk and looked down at the body.

Clint heard the warning from inside the hotel, and then the sheriff said something and started for the door.

"Sheriff, no!" Clint shouted.

He was too late.

•   •   •

One step into the lobby was all Kylie needed from the sheriff. Without the slightest hesitation he pointed the Peacemaker and fired twice at the sheriff, who had no chance to realize what he'd stumbled into. The bullets tore into his chest and sent him flying out the door.

Kimnach sat in stunned silence as he watched Oldman go flying out of the hotel lobby. He'd thought that the sheriff's arrival would save him, but he'd underestimated Luke Kylie. Apparently, the man was just as vicious and ruthless as John Duggin, the man he worked for.

Kimnach swallowed hard.

Clint saw Oldman come flying out of the hotel and fall lifeless to the street, like a rag doll—only rag dolls weren't filled with blood. The man was obviously dead.

Clint drew his weapon and approached the hotel more carefully than the sheriff had. For one thing he had no real idea how many men were inside, and he had no intention of walking into a bullet the way the lawman had.

Kimnach didn't hesitate. There was a doorway off to his right, in the back wall, away from the man with the gun. He scurried out from behind the desk and through the door. Hopefully, it would lead to a back—and why hadn't he thought of that before?

Kylie heard Kimnach move and looked up just in time to see the man rush out from behind the desk.

"Damn!" he swore. He came out from behind the sofa on a hopping run. His ankle felt on fire. He saw the doorway Kimnach had gone through and swore again. The man had finally thought about a back door.

He rushed through the door after his prey.

Clint heard footsteps from inside the hotel, moving away from him. Staying low he rushed into the hotel, finding what he had expected to find. The lobby was empty. He looked around for a back door and found it. Obviously, they'd gone out that way.

He turned and went back outside to check on the sheriff, even though he hadn't even the faintest hope that the man was still alive.

Kimnach went out the back door and then stopped. If he ran it would only be a matter of time before they caught him. He decided to stand and fight. He turned, put his back to the wooden fence that was behind the hotel, and decided to wait for the man to come out the door after him.

Kylie stopped just short of running through the back door. What if Kimnach was outside, waiting? And there was no window to go out this time.

Slowly, he inched his way to the door and stopped right next to it, his back to the wall. He held his breath and listened. Sure enough, from outside he heard the sound of a man breathing hard.

It would end here, one way or another.

THIRTY-SEVEN

The sheriff was dead, and so was the other man on the street. Clint heard footsteps approaching and looked up, gun ready. He saw Henry Whiteoak approaching, with a gun in his hand.

"Whiteoak! I figured you'd be long gone by now," Clint said.

"I almost was, but then I decided I couldn't just run out. Oh, God, that's Meade."

"He's dead, and so's the sheriff."

"Where's Kimnach?"

"Who?"

"Mike Kimnach. He was with Meade."

"I guess he's the man who was in the lobby. He went out the back door with somebody after him."

"Did you see who?"

"No," Clint said.

Just then there was another shot which made both men's heads jerk.

"Sounds like it's started up again," Clint said. "You want part of this?"

Whiteoak shrugged and said, "I don't think I have much of a choice."

"I'll go through the hotel, you go around the back."

"Right."

Both men moved, each wondering what they were going to run into.

Kylie took a deep breath and then launched himself out the door. This time he kept his finger off the trigger.

He hit the ground just as Kimnach fired, the shot going over his head. Because he was the less experienced of the two, Kimnach was outmatched. He would have been better off if he'd kept running.

Kylie squeezed off one shot, and it was enough. The bullet hit Kimnach square in the chest, flattening him up against the fence. As he slid down he left a trail of blood on the fence behind him.

"Yes!" Kylie said.

He got to his feet slowly and limped over to the body. He stared down at the dead man with satisfaction. This was going to make John Duggin very happy.

In response to all the shooting, Jeremiah Weller finally decided that he was probably missing all the action. He ran down the main street and heard where the commotion was coming from. He came within sight of the hotel just in time to see Whiteoak and Clint split up, only he didn't know who Clint was. He also saw the two bodies on the ground. He hurried over and satisfied himself that neither of them was Luke Kylie.

The action seemed to be shifting to behind the hotel,

so he slowly approached the door, satisfied himself that no one was in the lobby, and went in.

Kylie was looking down at Kimnach's body when he heard someone approaching from the alley. He turned, gun cocked, and waited.

Henry Whiteoak came running around the corner, gun in hand, and froze when he saw Kylie.

"Whiteoak!" Kylie said. "It's about time."

"Luke—" Whiteoak said.

"Don't—" Kylie started. He wanted to tell Whiteoak not to try anything stupid, because he knew Duggin wanted him alive, but he stopped short when another man came out the back door of the hotel.

With two against one, he had no choice but to shoot.

Clint heard voices in back of the hotel and decided he didn't have time to be careful. He went through the door and saw what looked like a standoff between Whiteoak and the man with the Colt Peacemaker.

"Damn," the man swore when he saw Clint, and swiveled to fire at him. Clint fired first, his bullet striking the man in the chest. The man took a step back, tripped over Kimnach's body, and went down.

He was dead when he hit the ground.

THIRTY-EIGHT

Standing inside the back door, Jeremiah Weller was able to hear the conversation that followed the demise of Luke Kylie. . . .

"I guess I owe you my life again, Clint," Whiteoak said.

Clint didn't reply. He walked to the two men and leaned over them. Both were dead.

"Tell me who they are."

"Sure," Whiteoak said, coming over to stand beside him. "The man you just killed was Luke Kylie. He's worked with John Duggin for years. The other man was my friend, Mike Kimnach."

"Maybe you should give Halsey his money back," Clint said.

Whiteoak shook his head.

"It's too late for that."

"The sheriff's dead, Whiteoak. There's no law in this town to protect you now, if Duggin is here."

"If he's here, then Weller is with him."

"You'd better get out."

"I don't dare go to the livery for my wagon."

"Just grab a horse and ride."

Whiteoak made a face.

"I'm no horse thief."

Clint laughed, in spite of the situation.

"What's so funny?"

"You cheat people out of their money, but you won't steal a horse?"

"Okay, so it's funny," Whiteoak said, "but I'm a con man, not a common thief."

"Well, then, we'd better get you a horse."

"Clint?"

"What?"

"You'd have a chance with Duggin."

"Forget it."

"Maybe if you just told him you were the Gunsmith, he'd leave."

"I said forget it."

"But . . . they killed Meade and Kimnach . . . and the sheriff."

"This man killed them," Clint said, "and he's dead."

"They'll find me."

"You should have thought of that before you decided to con Joe Halsey."

"You're a hard man."

"A hard man wouldn't have saved your life," Clint said, "twice."

Whiteoak looked down at the gun in his hand, and then holstered it.

"Third time might be the charm," he said, "for Duggin."

•   •   •

Jesus, Weller thought from the hallway of the hotel, the Gunsmith! And he'd already killed Kylie. Weller had no intention of going up against the Gunsmith. Nobody could pay him enough money to do that.

He knew what he had to do. He had to get to Duggin. He'd want to know that a man like Clint Adams had taken a hand in this. There was no point in getting himself killed when he had to warn Duggin.

Easing back down the hall, the man broke into a run when he reached the lobby. He ran out the front door, pushing through the crowd that had gathered around the bodies of the two dead men.

THIRTY-NINE

"You chicken-shit little prick!"

Duggin's outburst caused Weller to flinch.

"I should kill you now."

Duggin was not pleased at the news that Luke Kylie was dead. Not even the knowledge that both Kimnach and Meade were dead could change that, not while Whiteoak was still out there.

"There wasn't nothin' I could do," Weller said. "Kylie was dead when I got there."

"Sure, after he did his job and killed those two," Duggin said. "You, on the other hand, could have had the drop on Whiteoak, but instead you ran—"

"But that's what I came back to tell ya," Weller said. "Whiteoak wasn't alone."

That stopped Duggin.

"Who was with him?"

"Clint Adams."

Duggin didn't move, or say anything, or breathe at the news.

"You know, the Gunsm—"

"I know who he is, goddamn it!" Duggin said. "What the hell is the Gunsmith doin' with Whiteoak?"

"Well, it didn't sound like they was friends, but they did know each other before this. Whiteoak said this was the second time Adams had saved his life."

"You heard them talkin'?"

"That's right. I knew you'd want to know what they were—"

"What did they say?"

Weller gave Duggin every sentence, word for word, as the Killer listened intently.

"Then Whiteoak's not comin' here for his wagon."

"Didn't sound like it."

"And the lawman's dead?"

Weller nodded.

"Kylie killed him, too."

"Sounds like Kylie did a lot of your work for you, Weller," Duggin said.

Weller almost said that the same was true of Duggin, but he decided against it.

"What do we do?" Weller asked.

Duggin licked his lips.

"I can handle Adams."

"That would leave Whiteoak for me."

"Could you handle that?" Duggin asked with a sneer.

"Sure, Duggin—"

"But not here," Duggin said. "Not in town."

"Why not? The sheriff's dead."

Duggin shook his head.

"Listen to me. The whole town's gonna be in an uproar. What we have to do is leave town and wait for Whiteoak to do the same."

"And what about Adams?"

"If he leaves with Whiteoak, then he'll die, too."

Duggin was still licking his lips at the prospect of throwing down on Clint Adams. Killing the Gunsmith would give his own reputation a huge boost, and he figured Halsey would throw in a bonus. He'd just tell the rancher that Adams was working with Whiteoak.

Stroking the guns under his arms, Duggin actually grinned with anticipation. The look on his face both pleased and frightened Weller. It didn't look like Duggin was going to kill him, but it sure did look like the man had gone crazy, grinning like that.

"I've killed a lot of men in my time, Weller," he said. He put his hand on the other man's shoulder, causing Weller to flinch. "But I've never gunned down a legend . . . not yet, anyway."

The two men stood that way for a few moments, Weller afraid to move and disturb his boss's new mood.

Finally, Duggin removed his hand and spoke.

"Let's get to the horses, Jerry," he said. "It's time to leave town."

Duggin had never called Weller "Jerry" before. He didn't quite know if this was good or bad.

FORTY

Clint and Whiteoak went back to the Texas Grand Hotel after Clint told the crowd of people who had gathered around the bodies to have them moved to the undertaker's.

"Who's gonna be our sheriff now?" someone had asked.

"Talk to your mayor."

As they entered, Katherine came around the desk and ran to him, throwing her arms around his neck.

"Are you all right?"

"I'm fine," Clint said, "but five men are dead."

"My friends," Whiteoak said sadly.

"And the sheriff."

"Oh, no," Katherine said. "What about . . ."

"The man who killed them is dead, too," Clint said.

"What happens now?"

"Now," Clint said sourly, "Whiteoak leaves town before somebody else gets killed."

"Hey," Whiteoak said, "you can't blame me—"

"Sure I can," Clint said. "How many men are dead, Whiteoak, because you wanted to swindle Joe Halsey out of some money?"

Whiteoak didn't answer.

"I hope you got a lot of money out of that deal," Clint said. "You're going to need it to keep running."

"Why can't he just give the money back?" Katherine asked.

"He says it's too late for that."

Katherine stepped back and looked at both men.

"So what will he do?"

"He'll leave town, as soon as I can get him a horse." Clint looked at Whiteoak. "Stay here and don't go outside."

"But—"

"Just wait here!" Clint snapped.

"Clint . . ." Katherine said.

"I'll be right back," he assured her, and went out the door.

Clint was surprised to find the livery empty. He had half expected to run into Duggin and his other man.

From the looks of the stable floor, Duggin—or somebody—had been there for a while. There were the remnants of several cigarettes on the floor, and many footprints. Clint looked closely at the boot prints and decided that they'd been made by two different men. The way he reconstructed it, Duggin had been waiting for Whiteoak to come and get his wagon. When he heard all the commotion he decided to try for the professor another time.

But when, and where?

Clint went back to the hotel to tell Whiteoak he could have his wagon back after all.

• • •

"You mean he's gone?"

"It looks like it."

"And I can have my wagon?"

"Looks like it."

"What if he's waiting outside of town?"

"Which road?" Clint asked.

"What?"

"There are four ways out of town," Clint said. "You've got that many chances. If he's going to wait for you, he's got to pick one. So you pick one, and see who gets lucky, you or him."

"I'd be luckier if you came with me."

"I already told you, Whiteoak—"

"Okay, okay, never mind," Whiteoak said. "I guess I'll just have to take my chances."

"That's what I've been telling you."

"Ma'am," Whiteoak said, and went out the door.

"Wouldn't he have a better chance with you, Clint?" she asked.

"He's not my friend, Katherine," Clint said, "and he's brought all of this on himself. After all the men who have died because of him, why should he get away scot-free?"

"But can you send him out there, knowing he's going to be killed?"

He looked her in the eye and said, "Yes."

"And what about you?" she asked. "When will you be leaving?"

"Today."

She looked shocked.

"But . . . the tournament . . . the three thousand dollars. You know you'd win it—"

"I can't stay here, Katherine," he said. "I killed a

ınan and, except for you, this place holds no fascination or good memory for me. As for the three thousand, I'm ahead about twenty-two hundred dollars. I'll give you two thousand of that.''

''I couldn't take—''

''Sure you could,'' Clint said. ''You need it to keep this place going. Two thousand would do it, wouldn't it?''

''For a while, yes.''

''Then it's settled.''

''But you can't just give it to me . . . what if I made you a partner?''

He thought a moment, then said, ''A silent, absentee partner?''

''Done,'' she said.

''Good.''

''But couldn't you stay . . . one more night?''

''If I do, I might not get away for a while. The mayor here is bound to call for a federal marshal after everything that's happened.''

''Maybe he'll ask you to be sheriff—'' she suggested excitedly, but he cut her off before she could go any further than that.

''That would be even worse,'' he said. ''No, I have to leave.''

''All right,'' she said, ''I understand.''

''I'll just go upstairs and get my gear.''

''What about Whiteoak?''

''I'll just take a different road out of town than he does.''

''What if you run into this man Duggin?''

''I'll cross that bridge when I come to it.''

•   •   •

Katherine watched as Clint packed, and then they shared a passionate good-bye kiss. She wanted to plead with him to stay longer, but she decided to let him go. Maybe, someday, he'd come back this way and check on his two-thousand-dollar investment.

As he went out the front door, she wondered if she'd ever see him again.

When Clint got to the livery he was glad to see that Whiteoak's wagon was gone. From the tracks he left he could see that the man had headed north. That was fine with him, because he was going to saddle Duke and head south, back to Labyrinth, before more trouble found him.

FORTY-ONE

With Fort Wagner a day's ride behind him, Clint's anger was just beginning to subside. What had started out as a simple plan of drifting through western Texas had turned out to be a disastrous chain of events, all linked to Henry Whiteoak. He was happy now to have put Whiteoak and his problems behind him, and he refused to entertain any guilt at having left Whiteoak to his own devices.

As it turned out, Clint had a problem of his own. In the day since he'd left Fort Wagner his right hand had blistered from the burn he'd received from Luke Kylie's shotgun blast. He'd been able to use his gun during the time that followed the incident, but now, a day later, he could hardly close the hand around the butt of his gun. He supposed he should have seen a doctor before he left town, but he'd been in a big hurry to get out of there. Besides, he had never expected the injury to turn out so badly. Sure, he'd known that the hand had been burned, but he never expected this.

Sitting at his camp fire he tried pouring water on the hand, but that did little to help. The skin was stretched tight and very painful. Later, while cooking some bacon for dinner, he got the bright idea of smearing some bacon grease on the hand. That seemed to ease the tightness, but the hand still hurt, and he still couldn't hold his gun. He was lucky that he hadn't run into John Duggin after he left Fort Wagner. With his hand the way it was, he doubted he would have had much of a chance against the man—that is, if Duggin was even half what his reputation said he was.

He had cleaned up after his meal and poured himself some coffee when the back of his neck started to itch. His sixth sense was kicking in, telling him that someone was watching him. He didn't make an issue of it by looking around or making his suspicions obvious. The same sixth sense was telling him that he wasn't in any particular danger, that if someone was watching him they meant him no harm.

Clint didn't need to run into any more trouble, not with his hand in the condition it was in.

He walked over to where Duke was picketed and patted the big horse's neck.

"Looks like we're not going to get much sleep tonight, big fella," he said. "We're going to have to stay alert."

Clint took a quick look around, making it as casual as he could. His night vision was good, but he couldn't make anything out.

"Okay," he said to Duke, "let's see what happens when we bed down."

He walked back to the fire and rolled himself up in his blanket. Under the cover of the blanket he held his gun in his left hand and waited.

By the time the sun came up no one had sneaked into camp to visit him. Either his sixth sense had failed him this time, or whoever was watching him was truly doing just that, watching.

He made himself some fresh coffee, then broke camp and went to saddle Duke. His hand was worse today, and he was virtually one-handed in the task. He hoped that if someone was indeed watching him, they weren't watching *too* closely.

Once he had Duke saddled he swung aboard and started south.

Later in the day Clint was able to verify that he was being followed. It was his own damned fault for moving at such a slow pace. From the top of a rise he was able to make out the form of a wagon traveling behind him. As it turned out, his sixth sense had been working overtime. Nobody had been watching, but somebody was sure dogging his trail.

It was Henry Whiteoak.

Even though Whiteoak was a distance away, Clint could see the colors of his wagon. Was the man following him, or simply going in the same direction? The former seemed more likely, since Whiteoak had pulled out of Fort Wagner first and had *seemed* to be heading north. He must have doubled back, found Clint's trail, and started following it.

The flash of anger that Clint felt surprised him. At that moment he doubted that he had ever disliked a man as much as he did Henry Whiteoak.

He decided to wait right there for the man to catch up with him. Then he'd teach him a lesson.

FORTY-TWO

Henry Whiteoak was quite surprised when he came to the top of the rise and found Clint Adams sitting there, waiting. Duke, Clint's big gelding, was standing off to one side, grazing, and Clint himself was sitting at the base of a tree.

Caught in the act Whiteoak reined in his team and stepped down. His plan had been to trail Clint Adams until his temper cooled down, and then once again offer him a partnership.

"Well, Adams," he said, as Clint stood up and approached him, "how's life been—"

Whiteoak's greeting was cut short as Clint jabbed a heavy left into the man's midsection. Whiteoak staggered back and was just able to stay on his feet. He bent over, his hand to his gut, and tried to catch his breath.

"W-what was that for?" he stammered.

"You don't know?" Clint demanded.

"Well, I know you're mad—"

"Mad doesn't begin to cover it, Whiteoak," Clint

168

said. "What the hell do you mean by following me?"

Whiteoak held out a hand, indicating that he still needed a moment.

"I should beat you to a bloody pulp."

Whiteoak looked alarmed and backed up a few more steps, this time holding both hands out in front of him.

"Now wait," he said, "you don't understand—"

"What don't I understand?"

"Me," Whiteoak said, "you don't understand me."

"What's to understand?" Clint demanded. "You cheat people."

"Okay, so I cheat people," Whiteoak said. "I admit it, but I never killed anybody."

"And that makes it all right?"

"Look," Whiteoak said, "Duggin is the criminal, not me."

"You're just as much of a criminal as he is."

Whiteoak looked aghast.

"How can you say that?"

"You really don't believe it, do you?" Clint asked. "You really believe that what you do doesn't hurt people?"

Whiteoak looked totally baffled.

"All I do is steal money," he said. "People can make more money. Duggin kills people!"

"You stole money," Clint said, "and people paid for it with their lives."

"I didn't kill them!"

"You might as well have pulled the trigger yourself."

The two men stared at each other for a few moments, each seemingly at the end of their rope in trying to convince the other.

"Look," Clint said, "I don't think I can say this any clearer. Stay . . . the hell . . . away from me. Got it? I don't like you, and I never will. I never want to lay eyes on you again. Is any of this clear?''

"Sure," Whiteoak said, "sure, Clint, it's clear. You don't want to be friends anymore."

Clint opened his mouth and nothing but a croak came out. He tried again.

"We were never friends!"

"Sure, okay," Whiteoak said.

"I'm going to mount up and ride out," Clint said. "Don't follow me."

"I won't."

"If I catch you—"

"I said I won't! I give you my word."

Clint almost sneered—and he *never* sneered. He was glad that he managed to hold it back.

He walked to his horse, mounted up, and rode away without looking back.

Whiteoak watched him ride away, still puzzled over the man's words. What did he mean telling him he was as bad as John Duggin? My God, who *didn't* steal money at some time in one's life? Who was Adams, with his gunman reputation, to look down on him?

Hmm, Whiteoak thought, maybe they wouldn't have made such a good team after all.

FORTY-THREE

The Killer and Weller were on the con man's trail as soon as he left Fort Wagner. Obviously, the medicine man was too busy with something to check over his own shoulder.

"Why don't we take him now?" Weller asked.

"Because I want to see if he's gonna meet up with Clint Adams."

Weller shook his head. He couldn't believe that Duggin actually *wanted* to find Clint Adams.

"What makes you think he is?"

"He headed north, then doubled back and went south. If he's not meeting up with Adams, he's trying to find him, or trail him. I want to be there when he finds him."

I don't, Weller thought, but he knew if he tried to pull out now Duggin would kill him, so he stayed.

It took a day but Duggin watched with satisfaction as Whiteoak and Clint Adams had their meeting. From the looks of things, Adams wasn't too happy about it.

171

"They're fightin'," Weller said.

"Looks like it."

"What do we do?"

"I have a plan."

"Good."

"Just sit tight," Duggin said. "Let's see how this plays out."

They watched with interest while the two men talked, and then Clint Adams mounted up and rode off.

"We're gonna lose him," Weller said, secretly hoping he was right.

"Naw," Duggin said, "we won't. Come on."

"What are we gonna do?"

"We're gonna take Whiteoak."

"And what about Adams?"

"Don't worry," Duggin said, "he'll be back."

They spurred their horses on and rode hell-bent-for-leather after Henry Whiteoak.

Whiteoak was walking back to his wagon, still rubbing his tender stomach, when he heard horses approaching. For a moment he thought Clint Adams was coming back to apologize, but then he realized that there was more than one horse.

Suddenly, he realized he was in trouble. He looked back the way he had come and saw the two riders coming up the rise. He had no time to get his wagon moving, and even if he did he'd never outrun them. All he had time to do was take cover inside the wagon, which he did.

When the first shot came from the wagon it was wild. Duggin knew that Whiteoak was anything but a crack shot.

"He's shootin' at us!" Weller cried out.

What was your first clue? Duggin thought.

"We want him alive!" he reminded the other man. "Split up."

As the two men continued up the rise they started to split up, putting some distance between them. Whiteoak fired once again at each man, but he knew he had no chance unless Clint Adams heard the shooting and came to his assistance.

What were the chances of that?

Clint heard the shots and reined Duke in. There was no doubt in his mind what was happening. Duggin and his man had caught up to Whiteoak, who was now trying to fight them off. Two against one, and Whiteoak was no hand with a gun, unless they got close enough for him to pop off at them with that two-shot derringer.

"Ah, shit!" Clint swore, and turned Duke around.

FORTY-FOUR

They circled him and came at him from two directions. He had no chance, unless he could get them close enough to use the derringer.

Whiteoak tossed his rifle out of the wagon.

Duggin was surprised at Whiteoak's reaction to their flanking him. He didn't even have time to call out to him when the man's rifle came flying out of the wagon, striking the ground.

This was going to make it easier.

Duggin and Weller dismounted, and it was Weller who first heard and then saw Clint Adams riding up the rise from the other side.

"He's comin'!" he called out.

"I told you he would," Duggin said. "Whiteoak?"

"Yeah?"

"I want you to stay in the wagon," Duggin said, "but

174

if you have another gun in there you better toss it out now.''

Duggin waited a moment and then a handgun came flying out.

''Listen to me,'' Duggin said. ''If you don't come out, you won't get hurt. Halsey wants you alive.''

Sure, Whiteoak thought, so he can kill me himself.

Duggin crossed into Whiteoak's line of vision, but Whiteoak knew if he tried to use the derringer the other man would get him. He decided to wait for Clint Adams to reach them. Surely he was a match for both men.

Clint saw the two men standing alongside Whiteoak's wagon, looking like they were waiting for him. He assumed the tall, dark-clad man was John Duggin. He flexed his right hand and winced at the pain. He eased his gun out of his holster and stuck it into his belt, where he'd be able to reach it left-handed.

He didn't see Whiteoak anywhere, so he must have been inside the wagon, dead or alive—probably alive. A man like Joe Halsey would want to extract his own vengeance. Yeah, Clint thought, the others are dead and they're supposed to bring Whiteoak back alive.

Abruptly he reined Duke in and just sat there, waiting.

Duggin saw Clint Adams stop in his tracks, within hailing distance, but out of pistol range.

''Adams!''

''That you, Duggin?''

''I'm Duggin.''

''Where's Whiteoak?''

''In the wagon.''

''Alive?''

"So far," Duggin said. "Ride on up here, or he won't stay that way."

"Sure he will."

"What?"

"You want him that way."

"The hell you say."

"Your boss, he'll want Whiteoak alive."

"I'll kill him and enjoy it."

"Go ahead, then."

"Why'd he say that?" Weller asked Duggin.

"He's no friend of mine," Clint went on. "In fact, he's been a burr under my saddle since I met him. I don't care if you kill him."

"Jesus," Weller said. "Why don't we just let Adams go? We got Whiteoak."

"Shut up." To Clint he shouted, "You're bluffing."

"Try me," Clint said. "Go ahead and kill him."

As he was talking, Clint started to inch Duke closer. He knew he had stopped outside of pistol range, but his expert eye picked out a landmark that would put him in range—if he made a perfect shot.

"What do we do?" Weller asked.

"Shut up," Duggin said. "I've got to get him into range, that's all."

Duggin picked out a spot between himself and Adams and decided that if the man passed that point he'd be within range—if he made a perfect shot.

"Duggin—"

"I'm thinkin', damn it. Shut up."

Duggin pondered the problem as Clint kept inching Duke closer and closer to his landmark.

"I'll do it, Adams."

"Then do it, damn it! Get on with it so we can all leave."

"Weller."

"Yeah?"

"Walk over to the wagon with your gun out."

"Wha—"

"Like you're gonna kill Whiteoak."

"And then what?"

"When you're behind the wagon fire a shot."

"You think that will fool him?"

"We'll see. Go ahead, do it." He called out to Clint, "My man's gonna do it!"

"Well, come on. Get it over with."

"Do it!" Duggin snapped.

Listening to the conversation from inside the wagon, Whiteoak couldn't believe it. Clint was goading Duggin into killing him. Did the man dislike him that much?

As he listened, though, he realized that Duggin was sending Weller after him, remaining outside himself, probably to try to take Clint Adams—and Clint knew he had the two-shot derringer.

He snapped his wrist and the little gun leapt into his hand. Immediately his hand began to sweat, as he waited for Weller to appear.

Jeremiah Weller was muttering to himself.

"Gonna get out of this business as soon as I can," he was saying as he approached the wagon. "It's fulla crazy people."

He came around behind the wagon saying, "Fire a damn shot in the air, what the hell good is that? Should kill the sumbitch—"

He stopped when he saw the sumbitch pointing a derringer at him.

"Ah, shit," he said.

Clint was ready. He knew he had one advantage over Duggin. He was listening for the sound of the shot that little derringer would make. When Whiteoak fired, it would take Duggin a second to realize that the sound was from a derringer. That would give Clint the chance he needed to outdraw the man left-handed—and *then* he'd have to make that perfect shot.

Duggin watched as Clint Adams's horse kept moving closer and closer, seemingly by inches. Come on, big black, he thought, just another foot.

What was that?

There it was!

Clint drew his gun with his left hand and saw that Duggin's reaction was faster than he'd expected. Apparently, the man's expert ear had immediately picked up the sound of the derringer shot.

Duggin drew, and both men fired.

FORTY-FIVE

"Come in, come in."

Walking into Joe Halsey's office a twenty-five-year-old man was greeted by the land baron, shaking the beefy hand that was offered him.

"Have a seat," Halsey said. "I've heard a lot of good things about you."

The man sitting across from Halsey was young and full of ideas. Halsey had decided that checking out all the properties was too much work for him. For one thing his butt hurt from all the time in the saddle. So he'd decided to hire someone, but someone young who came with recommendations. Perhaps he could build himself a team of land scouts that he could totally trust.

This young man could be the first.

He'd been waiting a long time to hear from John Duggin, and he'd decided to simply get on with business as usual. Maybe it would take him a while, but Duggin would be back, and he'd have Whiteoak with him.

"So you think you can make me some money, eh?" Halsey asked.

"Oh, yes, sir," the man said. "I've been taught by the best, and I think I've got what you might call a Midas touch."

"Is that a fact? Wasn't that something about turning lead to gold?"

"Exactly."

"I like that in my employees."

The young man would be Joe Halsey's apprentice. He was cocky, and that was good, but he still had a lot to learn, and Joe Halsey was the man to teach him.

Across from Halsey, the young man was sitting with one hand in his pocket. In his palm was a charm that he carried for luck, given to him by the man who *had* taught him everything he knew.

The charm was a small glass bottle that had once been filled with a laudanum-tinged "miracle tonic." The last time he'd seen his teacher, the man had tossed him the bottle before heading off in a brightly colored wagon to try a new con as a "medicine man."

"For luck," Henry Whiteoak had said.

"But, Mr. Halsey," the young man said, "it takes money to make money."

"Don't you worry about that, son," Halsey said. "We're going to do just fine together. Yes, sir, just fine."

The young man sat back, smiled, and said, "I'm sure we will, sir."

"I told you we'd make a good team," Henry White-oak said.

He'd climbed down from the wagon after shooting Jeremiah Weller in the face, to see what happened between Duggin and Clint Adams. Amazingly, Clint had made a left-handed shot from what seemed to be too far away for any accurate pistol shot.

It was certainly too far for John Duggin, whose shot had missed.

Clint Adams, on the other hand, had made a perfect shot.

"Well?" Whiteoak said, pushing his luck. "Aren't we a perfect team?"

Clint stared at Whiteoak, still mounted on Duke, not sure what he was going to say. Finally, he decided to be brief.

"Like I said before, Whiteoak," Clint said. "I don't want to see you again."

He turned Duke around and headed south.

"Hey . . ." he heard Whiteoak calling. "Hey . . . what about these guys?"

"Bury 'em!" Clint snapped.

"Bury them?" Whiteoak said, looking down at the two dead men with a puzzled look. "Why?"

Watch for

BURIED PLEASURES

177th novel in the exciting GUNSMITH series
from Jove

Coming in September!